The Burning Woman

and other stories

The Burning Woman
and other stories

By

Frank Roger

evertype

2012

Published Evertype, Cnoc Sceichín, Leac an Anfa, Cathair na Mart, Co. Mhaigh Eo, Éire. www.evertype.com.

First edition 2012.

A catalogue record for this book is available from the British Library.

ISBN-10 1-904808-91-3
ISBN-13 978-1-904808-91-6

Set in Dutch Mediaeval and Imprint MT Shadow by Michael Everson.

Cover: Michael Everson.
Photo by Desy Pistonami, dreamstime.com/Leda_d_info.

Printed by: LightningSource.

Contents

The Burning Woman

and other stories

Irretrievably lost

G reg threw a glance at his watch as the aircraft started its descent. Strange, he thought, we're still an hour away from our destination. Perhaps the flight was ahead of schedule? A full hour ahead of schedule? That seemed hardly likely.

Yet the passengers were asked to fasten their seat belts as they would be landing in fifteen minutes' time. Well, maybe the hour of arrival on his travel documents had been wrong. Anyway, the aircraft was clearly going down fast, judging from the popping of his ears.

Fortunately the descent and the landing were uneventful. A few minutes later the passengers could leave the aircraft. To Greg's surprise, all of them followed the Transit signs, and he was the only one heading for the Baggage reclaim area.

A few moments later he ended up in a starkly lit hall, feeling somewhat uneasy. It felt so unnatural to be alone here, and the perfect silence was eerie. He walked over to the only baggage belt and waited until it would start moving. It didn't, and no bags showed up.

He stuck around for about fifteen or twenty minutes, and then sighed with despair. It was clear his bag was lost. It had happened before, but this time it felt particularly disagreeable. He looked around, saw a desk in the far corner, with a sign reading Handling Service, and headed that way.

"Can I help you, sir?" the woman behind the desk asked.

"My bag didn't show up," he said.

"Can I see the baggage label on your boarding pass?"

He handed her his boarding pass and she checked a few things on her computer screen. She frowned, turned her attention back to him and said: "According to my data, everything is perfectly all right, sir. You were on a flight from Birmingham to Aylmerville. Your baggage was checked in for Aylmerville, and should have arrived there."

"What do you mean?" he asked dumbfounded.

"It means that you're baggage isn't lost, sir. It was delivered in Aylmerville, which was your destination."

"But it didn't show up here on the belt."

"That's because this isn't Aylmerville," she explained. "Don't you understand, sir? Your bag isn't lost. You are."

"I beg your pardon?" he stammered. "If this isn't Aylmerville, then where am I?"

"I'm afraid I can't tell you, sir. This is no regular airport. It's a sort of emergency technical maintenance centre. Passengers are not supposed to show up here. This is for authorized staff and their equipment only. But every once in a while there's a glitch in the system."

"So what do I do now?"

She shrugged and said: "There are procedures for lost baggage, but not for lost passengers."

He stared at her, unable to utter a word.

"You're irretrievably lost, sir. The chances of this sort of thing happening are so negligibly small, that there's no procedure for it. I'm sorry, sir."

"But what am I supposed to do now?"

She flashed him a professional smile, and said: "I'm afraid I can't help you, sir. Have a nice day."

After her last word she turned her attention back to her work. His case had been closed.

Greg realized it was pointless to insist. He turned around and did a tour of inspection of the hall, but found only two locked doors. He couldn't go back to where he had come from either. He walked back to the desk, but it was closed now too and the woman had left. Maybe she had finished her shift.

He tried to make a few phone calls, but proved unable to reach anyone.

I'm stuck here, he realized. I'm irretrievably lost, like a piece of baggage that is never found again. It looks as if I'll spend the rest of my life in this empty hall—and that may not be all that long.

No one will find me here, however hard they look for me. It should be my luck that I end up being one of those extremely exceptional cases of lost passengers.

But there's one positive side to this, he thought. At least my baggage arrived at its destination safe and sound.

The question

Vincent was admiring the dome of Florence's cathedral as someone tried to attract his attention. He looked down and saw it was an old woman who had grabbed his arm with her clawlike fingers. He was struck by the contrast between her dirty, rumpled clothes and her eyes that burned with a feverish glow. In thickly-accented English she said: "Ask me any question about yourself, and for five euros I'll give you the answer. Only one question. Not more. Make sure it's an important question."

"Any question about myself? An important one? For five euros?" On the spur of the moment Vincent decided to go with the idea. "Well, all right then. How long will I live?"

"Are you sure that's the question you want to ask? You should know you'll have to live with the reply. Do you realize what that means?"

"Oh, come on," Vincent said, about to lose his patience with the woman. "You said you'd give the answer to any important question about myself. This subject happens to be important to me. Well?"

Her eyes bored into his, and he could almost feel the fervour burning within her. For a moment he felt a bit giddy.

"As you wish," she finally said. "I will tell you. You will die within a few months."

"Really? Now that's interesting. How will I die? What makes you so sure? Is there anything I can do about it?"

She shook her head. "Only one question. I'm sorry if you don't like the answer. You might have foreseen this problem and asked another question. Now of course it's too late. Can I have my five euros please?"

He handed her a five-euro note and walked off. He was only for a few days in Florence and wanted to see as much of the city's attractions as possible. He forgot about the woman and concentrated his efforts on what should be a fascinating exploration.

⌗

Vincent made his final stroll through the historical centre of Florence before going back to his hotel to check out and leave for the airport. As he walked towards the Piazza della Signoria he almost bumped into the old woman who had told him his future yesterday. He shot her an expectant glance, wondering whether she would recognize him and recall what she had told him. Her blank stare probably meant that to her he was just another tourist she might wrangle five euros from, if he were willing to make use of her fortune telling talents.

Then she looked up at him and said: "Ask me any question about yourself, and for five euros I'll give you the answer. Only one question. Not more. Make sure it's an important question."

"All right," he replied. "How long will I live?"

She looked into his eyes for a moment and then said: "You will die in your eighties, after having realized all your ambitions. You will live a full and satisfying life."

"Really? Well I'm glad to hear it. You know, yesterday I asked you the same question and you said I'd die within a few months."

"Yes," she said, "I remember it well. But the very fact that I told you that changed your future. You shouldn't have asked that question, as I had warned you. There are more worthwhile questions to be asked. You see, the knowledge of your early death will influence your lifestyle, even if unconsciously. It will lead you to be more careful, to take fewer risks, and thus you will avoid your early death. You will rewrite your own future thanks to this foreknowledge."

"Really? So in the end I did the right thing after all. I asked the right question. I saved myself from an early death."

She shook her head. "You don't think this through. The knowledge you just acquired about your longer life expectancy will in its turn affect your lifestyle and make you rewrite your future once again. You don't understand the string of rapid changes you set in motion. Can I have my five euros please? Actually I think I'm entitled to a bit more. I replied to more than one question."

He handed her a five-euro note and said: "You know, you have a strange way of making a living, telling people to ask you a question about themselves and then treating them to replies ringing with crackpot philosophy. Wouldn't you agree there are easier jobs that pay a bit more around here? Look, I'll give you an extra five euros. Have a nice day."

He handed her another banknote, turned around shaking his head, and stepped off the pavement. He didn't even see the bus that came rushing on until he was under its wheels.

The winds of unchange

This must be the place, Henry thought. He parked his car at the side of the road, got out and slowly climbed the hill that had been described to him so many times. At last he would be able to check for himself if there was any truth to the stories people told about this "phantasmagorical" site, where everything supposedly was constantly in motion, where change was the only constant. Most rationally-thinking people had always shrugged off the fantastic stories about the site as examples of superstitious folklore, products of the imagination appealing only to the simple-minded, to persons easily given to flights of fancy in an effort to escape the grey monotony and endless tedium of everyday life. However, he would be the first to point out that rationally-thinking people should apply the empirical method to verify any wild story's validity. From a scientific viewpoint, beliefs based on preconceived notions and prejudice were as unacceptable as beliefs based on superstition.

He had now reached the top of the hill and let his eyes roam across the landscape sprawling at his feet. A meadow, dotted with shrubs and trees, sloped gently downward. A hundred metres away from his vantage point, a narrow river cut a swathe through the greenery, and still further away the shrubs and trees thickened into a forest covering the upward slopes leading to the mountain range at the edge of his vision.

Henry noted there were no animals to be seen, exactly as he had been told. Animals instinctively felt there was something wrong with this place, the rumour went, and avoided it at all cost. Indeed, he saw no birds winging past in the sky, no squirrels scurrying about, not even any insects buzzing or fluttering around. The place was ominously quiet.

Why don't we take a closer look, Henry thought, and started walking down the slope. A feeble wind ruffled his thinning blond hair. So far everything seemed to be pretty calm and normal. So where were the dizzying changes this landscape was supposed to be going through? The meadow, the water glistening in the early summer sun, the forest in the distance, the blue sky and the few wisps of cloud didn't seem to be subject to any change. Apart from the absence of animals, as far as this could be detected by merely looking around, there was nothing special about the place.

Harvey shook his head. He should have known. Had he really expected to run into magical transformations here? The normalcy of his surroundings merely confirmed what he had thought about the entire affair all along. Still, now that he had gone to the trouble to come over here, he might as well stroll around a bit and enjoy the beauty and the quietness of the place.

He flicked back his unruly dreadlocks, forced into a ponytail, onto his back and descended further down the slope. This would be an ideal place for a picnic, he thought. Down here there was virtually no wind, and it was quite warm. He took off his corduroy jacket, and set course for the river. The faint gurgling of the water was the only sound breaking the silence.

Harry scanned the landscape in all directions, but nothing had changed ever since he had arrived: the meadow, the river, the forest on the mountain slopes in the distance, the blue sky, the absence of animals. He closed his eyes for a moment, enjoying the energizing sensation of the sun beating down on his clean-shaven head. This place may not harbour any magic, he thought, but it's quite wonderful all the same. He took off his boots and socks and stepped into the cool water. It felt so refreshing that he decided to take off his pants and underwear and his chequered shirt as well, and splashed around for a few minutes in the waist-deep water.

Well, Hector thought as he climbed back onto the grass, it's about time I went back. He waited until his body had dried, and used his T-shirt to towel off his mane of waist-length jet-black hair. Then he pulled on his kilt, slipped his feet back into his sandals, and threw his bearskin coat around his shoulders.

Slowly he walked back up the hill he had come from. When he had reached the top, Horace turned around and cast one final glance at the landscape behind him. The meadow, the river, the forest and the mountains were still as they had been ever since he had gotten here, and probably hadn't changed in ages. He chuckled, and shook his head. Superstitious, simple folk! At least now he could cast aside their wild claims with the argument that he knew better, because he had been there, he had seen "with his own eyes" what it was really like.

Horvath quickly descended the hill to where he had parked his car. He got in and threw his coat and the wet T-shirt on the back seat. Strange, he thought. He wasn't sitting comfortably, as if someone a lot shorter than he had readjusted the seat while he was away. He pushed the seat back to its regular position, and started the engine. To his surprise, the pedals somehow didn't seem to be where his feet were used to finding them. Perhaps his feet were swollen because of his skinny-dipping in the cool water?

These minor discomforts were quickly forgotten, however, and presently Horvath was on his way back home, glad that he had seen his ideas based on rational thought confirmed.

The fairground attraction

A rthur had almost finished his tour of the fairground when a man attracted his attention and said: "Visit the house with an infinite number of storeys. Walk up the stairs, go through room after room, and you'll see that there is no top floor. Don't just believe me, go and look for yourself."

The man pointed to the construction behind him. Arthur smiled and shook his head. This house-shaped fairground attraction could not have more than four or perhaps five storeys. No doubt optical tricks or mirrors were used to create the illusion of a seemingly endless succession of flights of stairs.

"You appear doubtful," the man said. "Why don't you see for yourself? You'll soon discover that I'm right. It'll only cost you a tenner."

Arthur hesitated for a moment, then decided to give it a try. After all it might be fun to find out how the illusion was achieved.

"All right," he said, and groped in his pocket for the money. "I'll go and take a look up there."

"Thank you," the man said, accepting his money with a big smile. "This way, please."

He walked through the door that was held open for him and found himself in a small windowless room. A short flight of stairs led to the second floor. He climbed it and arrived in a room identical to the first one, with stairs leading to the third floor. Behind him a door swung shut. He checked the doorknob and found it was locked. There was no going back down. The only way to go was up.

He continued until he arrived at the sixth floor, and halted to think for a while. So far all the rooms (windowless, without exception) and stairs had been identical, and each time he had

10

climbed a staircase a door had blocked the way back down for him. Everything had appeared quite normal, and he hadn't seen a trace of an optical illusion of any sort. Yet there was no way this structure could have six floors, with a seventh one up there at the top of the stairs.

Well, there's only one way to find out, he concluded. Let's climb as far up as I can, and look out for any details that might give away the true nature of this thing. And let's count the number of floors.

When he arrived on the twelfth floor he started to grow suspicious. On the twentieth floor his suspicion slowly gave way to fear. On the thirty-fifth floor his fear turned into panic. On the fortieth floor he found he'd had enough, and wanted to go back down. He tried to open the door leading to the stairs behind him, but even when he resorted to brute force, the door didn't yield.

He took his mobile to call for help, but to his dismay he had no service. He was left to his own devices here, with no other option than to keep climbing staircase after staircase. He knew there had to be a logical explanation for this illusion, but it escaped him completely.

So he kept climbing, passing through room after room, going up flight after flight of stairs. On the fifty-seventh floor he took a short break, wishing he had been thoughtful enough to take a bottle of water with him. He was growing thirsty and tired, but there was no point in staying here. If there was an exit, it should be on the top floor. But then again, this house was supposed not to have a top floor. Anyhow, he would find out at one point.

He kept going. He started getting really desperate on the seventy-fourth floor, and when he reached the ninety-third floor he just couldn't continue anymore and collapsed at the bottom of the stairs leading to the next floor.

⌗

Yesterday at the fairground's closing time, a man was found in one of the attractions. He turned out to be severely dehydrated and unconscious, and was rushed to the hospital where he is expected to make a full recovery.

The attraction was closed by the police, and the incident will be thoroughly investigated. The owner of the attraction, a house-like structure giving the illusion of having an endless number of floors, declared that all safety precautions had been taken and that no accident had happened ever before.

"I just don't understand what went wrong," he stated. "This man was found on the third floor, just below the top level. Now it's true that the optical illusions used in the building are extremely convincing and may be unsettling to some, but that doesn't explain the victim's serious condition. I'm sure the investigation will prove that my attraction is perfectly safe, and I hope to be open for business again as soon as possible."

The police are declining to comment until they have the results of their examination.

The end of time

It's time to go now, Roderick thought. I'm ready. There's no point in staying up here. The end is near.

He cast a final glance at the street and the people walking on the sidewalk or driving along. Didn't any of them know what was about to happen? Was he the only one who had received information from above about the impending catastrophe?

It didn't really matter. He was among the privileged who would survive. It was not up to him to decide who else would.

He made his way to the old nuclear shelter, a relic from the cold war of bygone days that some people had urged him to tear down as it no longer served a purpose. Fortunately he had not listened to them. The shelter would now prove far from useless.

Yesterday he had checked if he had enough supplies of food and water. He also had a nice library down there, as well as candles and matches just in case things got really bad.

He went down, switched on the emergency lights and closed the door behind him. He ensconced himself in an old comfortable chair he had dragged down here and checked his watch. If he had interpreted the information correctly, there would still be a few hours of peace and harmony before all hell broke loose.

The Apocalypse. It had been in the air. Honestly, he had not been surprised to receive the news from above that the end of time was near. And he had been relieved to find himself among the privileged who would survive it all. It was a reward for a life led according to the rules. He had known all along that it was wise not to stray from the right path.

All there was left to do now was wait for the inevitable. He tried to read a bit, but wasn't quite in the mood and dozed off.

When he awoke he checked his watch to see how long he had been asleep and found to his dismay that it was no longer working. He should have replaced the batteries before coming down here. Was there another way to find out what time it was? This was important, as he had to know when the Apocalypse would hit humanity.

His radio! He looked around for it and then remembered it was still in the house upstairs. He had concentrated on food, water and books, but in his hurry he had neglected a few other vital things.

I'll quickly go back up and get all the stuff I forgot, he thought. Let's hope it's not too late, that the Apocalypse has not yet descended upon us. I just need that radio. It'll be my only link with the outside world. And my cell phone, shouldn't I take that too? Now he had never liked all that modern stuff, but it might come in handy now.

He wanted to open the door but it appeared stuck. He kept trying, using all his force, convinced that it would yield if only he pushed hard and long enough. After a few minutes he gave up, panting with exhaustion.

It's my own fault, he realized. I should have kept this shelter in good repair. But how could I have foreseen I would need it one day?

He sat down and let his thoughts roam. He was truly cut off from the outside world now. There was just no way for him to track the passing of time, to find out what was going on out there.

He glanced once again at his watch. Wait a second, he thought. I received news that the end of time was coming. Naturally I assumed this was the Apocalypse, but what if it simply meant that my watch would stop?

He shook his head, rejected the idea right away. Why would he receive news from above about something so trivial as his watch? That didn't make any sense. Unless of course the watch grinding to a halt was merely a symbol for a much grander event?

There just was no way to find out anything without leaving the shelter, and he was unable to do so or to get in touch with someone outside who might help. All he could do was wait, whether the Apocalypse was raging outside or not.

So it doesn't really matter, he concluded. I'll be stuck in here until my supplies run out. One way or another, that will be the end of time for me.

Another fortnight of peace

I get outside in the harsh sunlight, squinting, and hear Harry call my name from across the street. I wave my hand, and cast a glance in his direction.

"Well, what do you say?" he asks, running a hand through his thinning hair. He is panting, his enormous bulk heaving with the exertion of the work he has apparently just finished. He is a fat man, but good-natured, basically amiable. Good thing to have him in the neighbourhood.

"Marvellous!" I call back. "Fine piece of craftsmanship! That'll do the job, Harry!" I nod approvingly and give him the thumbs-up. Harry smiles his usual extra-wide smile, casts some inquiring glances upwards as though there is something wrong with the blue expanse of the sky, then disappears inside his house. He has put in some really solid work this time around: he has gone so far as to cover up the windows with a solid line of bricks and has barricaded the door completely. His house now has the appearance of a bunker. Well, yes, as a rule Harry *does* tend to exaggerate. Bricking up the whole thing is highly effective of course, but tomorrow he'll have to pull it all down again, unless he chooses to keep on living in a bunker. But then again, let us be honest: last time he simply boarded up everything with heavy-duty planks which turned out to be quite insufficient. He suffered considerable damage, and quite a lot of stuff was destroyed or taken away. That's the kind of thing that gets to a man, so let us not judge Harry too quickly.

I for my part have closed up all entrances with somewhat less drastic means, just like last time around. Back then we didn't have any serious problems, only some minor damage which was quickly repaired.

16

I let my gaze roam across the street: here and there someone is putting the finishing touches to his defences: steel shutters, solid brick walls, armoured concrete constructions, live barbed wire, the whole gamut of things. A pattern is becoming apparent in recent times: shopkeepers, like Harry, show an increasing tendency towards elaborate defence lines, in some cases reaching over-the-top proportions. So Harry's sportswear shop may look like a bunker, but then shift your gaze to Mr Rosenblum's jewellery store and let us compare notes. What can we expect next? The moat-and-drawbridge approach? Burning oil? I am being cynical now, and some would contend my cynicism is unjustified. These are serious issues, they would say. And, quite honestly, they would be right. So please ignore my sarcasm.

Everyone is about finished by now, these activities having become a routine into which we smoothly slip back when the time has come. I finish my own activities, admire the result of my labour not unlike an artist beholding his latest creation. I inhale the invigorating fresh summer air for the last time, look at the clear blue sky for the last time before I get back in (now I think I understand Harry's reaction) and then I too make my retreat. Not until tomorrow, around noon, will we surface again.

In the evening and all through the night we try to ignore the noise and pretend to be in deep concentration over our books and magazines. But Miranda seems to be staring at the very same page all night long and I am turning a page at regular intervals merely to keep up a semblance of normalcy and young Kim isn't even bothering to attempt anything resembling normal behaviour. Obviously no one is willing to admit this, but the noise up there is absorbing all our attention. Wailing sirens, droning engines, squealing tyres, the nerve-wracking chop-chop-chop of low flying helicopters. Gunshots and explosions. Shattered glass (despite all our efforts? It seems barely conceivable!), excited and/or inciting yells, screams of agony, catcalls and outbursts of joy. Heavy droning, dull thuds, metallic clashes. The night seems to drag on endlessly, a kaleidoscope of sound out of control. Sleep isn't even considered; it has become an element of the past overnight. Or, if I may rephrase, of the future—tomorrow to be more precise.

17

As morning extends into noon our nervous systems are finally given some respite. Silence begins to take possession of the street, a silence that appears to grow all-pervasive. We wait for a little while longer, just to be on the safe side, then I leave the cellar and climb back up to the surface. Everything has withstood the onslaught, there isn't even any minor damage. I am flooded with a feeling of relief.

After some time I manage to open up the doorway. The street is a terrible mess, a modern day battlefield. Across the street I spot Harry, already hard at work at pulling down his brick bulwark. What an immense amount of work for one single day! It has however turned out to be quite effective, which is what it was all about of course. Harry becomes aware of my presence, waves at me and yells, "What a mess!"

"Hell of a mess!" I shout back.

"Well, what do you say?" he asks, pointing at his fortifications, beaming with pride and satisfaction.

"Solid piece of craftsmanship," I answer. "No getting through."

Harry grins approvingly, spits in his hands, gets back to pulling down the layers of bricks. More and more people are coming out. Casual greetings are exchanged. Everything is quickly checked for damage, but all this has become a routine by now and most fortifications appear to meet the desired standards.

Looks of disapproval are cast across the ruined streetscape, pockmarked as it is with bomb craters, burned-out vehicles, lumps of stone and asphalt and concrete and metal. Some way off there's the glinting carcass of a crashed helicopter, like the lifeless chitinous armour of an irritating insect which was slapped down. Casualties have of course been taken away during the night as usual.

Everyone starts tearing down his barricades and fortifications. We have two weeks to breathe freely now. Then this madness will start all over again and we'll have to get moving again. There will be another soccer game in a fortnight and another gargantuan battle will be waged between the fans and the forces of law and order in the streets of the city.

I cast a final glance at Harry who is working up a sweat and then I too start working on pulling down my fortifications. We will be allowed to do without for another fortnight.

The stranger who looked
hauntingly familiar

The old woman shot a warm smile to the fortyish man entering her room. She remained silent, and the expression on her face, gentle yet quizzical, made it clear she did not know him and left him the initiative to engage in conversation.

"Good afternoon," the stranger said. "How are you today? Is everything all right?"

She nodded politely, and finally added, "Fine, thank you," after a moment's hesitation, as if she had not spoken in years and it took her an immense effort to start the words flowing again.

"Is there anything you need?" the man asked, before the silence could return. "Do you have everything you want here?"

"Oh, I'm perfectly all right here," she answered. "The food is quite excellent, the staff is very kind and helpful, and I have my magazines and my TV to fill my time... Although there seems to be little that I find worth reading or watching these days." She shook her head, cast a glance at the TV in a corner of the room, as if to check if it was still there just in case she changed her mind.

"I prefer sitting here," she continued, "reminiscing about the good old days. I still vividly remember the time when my children were young, my husband was alive and well and a bright future seemed to be beckoning. Oh, how I wish those times could return. But I'm afraid that's not how things work." She sighed, staring at him without really seeing him, her attention focussed on memories that came flooding back from the farthest reaches of her mind.

"Oh, those were the days... My husband was an architect, and he used to work at home, which allowed us to have a rich family life. We were able to raise our children together, unlike most people. We had a daughter called Jessica, and a son called

20

Thomas. They were bright children, and turned out, unsurprisingly, to be fine students. They were an endless source of joy for us. We were a happy family, we really were. I have fond memories of all the holidays we spent together. Every summer we went to Spain or Italy or Greece, and other places that had beach resorts and sunshine where we could relax and our children could play.

"Then our children grew up, left the house and married. My husband and I looked forward to a happy old age together, but cancer took him away from me when he was sixty-two. That was over twenty years ago. I've been alone ever since. I'm doing fine here, as I said, but every so often I suffer from loneliness, and even from a feeling of loss, although I did learn to live with the hand fate dealt me.

"What hurts me most is that I never see my children anymore. I haven't seen them in ages. As a matter of fact, I often wonder what became of them. Are they still alive and well, where do they live, do they have successful careers, do they have children? Maybe I'm a grandmother, for all I know! Who knows how many grandchildren I have! Don't you think a grandmother is entitled to see her grandchildren a few times a year? Or am I really asking too much?" She shook her head, her face lined with stark despair, on the verge of breaking into tears.

"I don't even recall the last time they dropped by," she continued in a soft, trembling voice. "And I have no idea why they never visit me anymore. I'm still their mother, aren't I? They can't have forgotten about me, can they? Maybe something dreadful has happened! My God, I shouldn't think about it! The very idea drives me crazy. Oh dear, you probably think I'm losing my mind or something. I'm so sorry."

She fell silent, cast down her gaze, trying to regain control of her emotions. For a while she appeared lost in thought, then she looked back up at him, and said in a remarkably even voice: "I hope you don't mind me telling you all this. I know this doesn't make any sense, but somehow you remind me of my son Thomas. Your face seems so hauntingly familiar, although we don't know each other. And yet I have this uncanny feeling my son might closely resemble you. Although of course I have no idea what Thomas now looks like, as I haven't seen him in ages. So it must be my mind that's clouded, or my memories that are playing tricks on me. I hope you can forgive an old lady for reminiscing about her youth and aching to see her long lost son..." Her voice trailed off, and she appeared to drift back into the private inner world of her thoughts and recollections.

When the silence grew uncomfortable, the man said good-bye and left the room. The old woman didn't even look up.

As the man passed the *Golden Sunset*'s reception on his way out, the woman behind the desk asked him, "Oh, Mr Renneville, how's your mother?"

"I'm afraid she doesn't recognize me anymore," he said. "And every single time I pay her a visit, she tells me the same story about her children who have forgotten about her and how lonely she is." He sighed. "Well, it's been this way for years, and I don't think her condition is likely to improve."

"But still you keep coming. Doesn't that mean you keep hoping?"

"Yes, you're right, I still drop by twice a week, and so does my sister, but frankly, we've lost all hope of seeing mother becoming her old self again. We no longer bring the children along. It was too unsettling an experience for them, seeing their grandmother in this condition. But I suppose Jessica and I will keep visiting her until the end."

"I understand. See you on Thursday then, Mr Renneville. Good-bye."

"Good-bye," Thomas Renneville said, and left the *Golden Sunset*.

The disruption

"What are you doing here?" Gerry's older brother Jake asked. "I'm throwing pebbles into the sea as far as I can," Gerry replied. "Just look."

He picked up a pebble from the beach, took a few steps back, ran forward and flung away his projectile.

"Wow," he exclaimed. "Did you see where it came down? You couldn't even hear the splash."

Jake shook his head. "Haven't you got anything more interesting to do than wasting your time like this here? Shouldn't you think about school a bit more?"

"I don't like school."

"We all know that. You'll be sorry for neglecting your school duties, mark my words."

Gerry hated it when his brother Jake brought up this subject. Jake loved school in general and math in particular, and he was a brilliant student—none of which was the case with Gerry, who had other priorities in life. True, his parents preferred Jake's school track record to Gerry's obstacle course.

"Still, I'm not doing anything wrong here," Gerry said in his defence.

"I'm not so sure about that," Jake countered. "For how long have you been throwing pebbles into the water? How many have you flung out there by now?"

Gerry shrugged. "I don't know. But I've been doing this for a while."

"Oh, Gerry. You don't seem to realize what effect your actions may have."

"What are you talking about?"

"Let me explain. The pebbles you see here on the beach started out as pieces of rock. They became round pebbles through a process of erosion, after rolling across the bottom of the sea and drifting along on the currents for centuries or perhaps millennia, until they finally washed ashore here. This entire pebble beach has been in the making for ages, it's the result of a historical process we can barely fathom. And now you are throwing all these pebbles back where they came from in the space of a few days."

"So what?"

"Can't you see, Gerry? You're causing an abrupt reversal of an evolution that's been going on for a long time. That may well lead to a disruption of the natural flow of things. Who knows what terrible effects your stupid little game will have? What gruesome process have you set in motion?"

"You're kidding, right?" Gerry said after a short silence, then added doubtfully: "What might that disruption be?"

"We'll probably find out when it's too late," Jake said. "It could be anything. Anyway, don't say you weren't warned. Keep in mind what I just told you. And think a bit more about school."

Jake wandered off and Gerry thought about what his brother had told him. Had he been serious? Could throwing pebbles back into the sea have disastrous consequences? It seemed like a silly idea to him, but then again his brother Jake hardly ever made jokes. Gerry didn't know what to think of his "warning". This couldn't be true, right? Still, he didn't trust it.

❖

A few days later Jake walked up to Gerry again at the beach. His older brother couldn't believe what he saw.

"What the hell is this supposed to mean, Gerry? What are you doing?"

"I'm throwing back as many pebbles as I can," he explained. "I must have returned a hundred by now, and the rest will follow. I can't wait to see the effect."

"The effect? What effect?"

24

Gerry paused for a moment, stared his brother in the eyes. "Don't you know what happened in Crescent Meadows College yesterday?"

Jake thought and nodded. "Yes. There was a light tremor and a few classes were evacuated because cracks had appeared in the walls. The damage was only superficial, I believe. So?"

Gerry held up the pebble he clutched in his palm. "That must be the disruption you told me about. Apparently it wrecks school buildings. I just didn't throw back enough pebbles for it to have its full effect, but I'm seeing to that now."

Jake shook his head in disbelief. "Gerry, you're out of your mind. Stop this nonsense, or there will be nothing left of this pebble beach."

"Nor of any of the schools in the area," Gerry replied.

He threw away the pebble he held, and immediately picked up another one.

"Now leave me alone," he told Jake. "I've got important work to do."

A new world record

"We made it to the top!" Takumi exclaimed ecstatically. He checked his watch and added: "We went from sea level to the top of Mount Everest in exactly one hour and fifteen minutes."

"A new world record," his friend Giancarlo cried out. "We did it! We did it!"

"We should admit that the sea level having risen drastically in the last few decades gave us an advantage over our predecessors," Takumi countered, pointing at their boat, moored to an outcrop of rock in the water below, easily within visual range.

"That's true, but it doesn't change the fact that we went from sea level to the top of Mount Everest in a record time," Giancarlo pointed out. "We did establish a new world record."

"Absolutely right," Takumi admitted. "We can rightly be proud of our achievement. Now shouldn't we begin our descent?"

"You're right, let's go."

The two men started their descent to the place where they had moored their boat, from where they would go back to their floating village, eager to tell their story of their new world record.

The good example

"You know, Susan," Uncle Geoffrey told me, "I've been thinking about something that was on TV."

"Oh, and what was that?" Uncle Geoffrey usually invited me on Saturday afternoon for a coffee at his favourite pub downtown, and then he talked at length about one of his pet topics. My uncle is a retired military man, and we hardly share any interests or opinions. He sipped his coffee, squinted against the sunlight coming in through the window and said:

"There's been a lot of coverage on TV lately of the various wars raging all over the world. They keep talking about the atrocities, the horror, the sheer barbarity."

"Oh, yes." My uncle tends to address issues that are related to his days in the armed forces. He knows I have little fondness for such matters, and I wondered why he had chosen to bring up this particular issue. Perhaps he felt he had something really important to say on the subject.

"You see, Susan, war is always presented as a horrible thing. And of course it is, it's just that there's a positive side to it as well, which never gets much attention."

"What's the positive side of war, then?" I asked, bracing myself for one of his typical diatribes.

"War keeps the population figures down. There's just too many of us around. Our planet can't handle six billion human beings or more, there just aren't enough natural resources, there's not enough living space. War is man's way to check this uncontrolled growth. It's a form of population control. Think about it, Susan."

I thought for a moment and decided to play along with his game. "But despite all the wars that are raging everywhere, our population figures keep rising. It's clear war alone is not enough

27

to decimate mankind. Even the two World Wars didn't make a dent in the global figures. I believe we should take additional measures."

"What are you trying to say, Susan?" A deep frown appeared on my uncle's forehead. I definitely had his attention.

"Don't they say that more people are killed in traffic accidents than in armed conflicts? I think that offers us a few possibilities."

Uncle Geoffrey stared at me, clearly at a loss for words.

"We might abolish the speed limit," I suggested. "That should raise the number of fatal accidents. And of course, safety belts will have to go too. They only prevent people from surviving crashes."

"Are you serious?" Uncle Geoffrey whispered, hardly believing his ears.

"We could do even more," I continued. "We might stop taking care of victims with grave injuries. Why don't we simply close the hospitals? Ban all medicine, stop treating the sick and the wounded. That way we should get rid of a nice bunch of people. And only the strongest ones will survive. Not only do we end up with fewer people, but also with a superior lot. You see, I think you were right, there's too many of us around and we have to do something about it. So, how do you like my suggestions? Are you with me?"

Uncle Geoffrey shook his head. "But Susan..." was all he managed to say. It was clear my reasoning had upset him, even if I had merely elaborated on his ideas. He obviously hadn't expected such drastic measures from his niece. Young women didn't think and talk like that.

After an uncomfortable silence, Uncle Geoffrey tried to steer the conversation back into more tranquil waters, but the mood had been broken. So it didn't come as a surprise that he said it was nice to have spent some time together, but that he really had to go now. He promised to call me again to have a chat sometime soon, paid the bill and said good-bye.

As he was about to cross the street, he turned around to wave at me, and didn't see a car coming his way at very high speed. He managed to jump aside at the very last moment; the car missed him by a few centimetres and rushed off.

"Did you see that?" he cried out, furiously. "That guy could have killed me."

"Perhaps that was the idea," I replied.

Baffled, he said: "What's that supposed to mean, Susan?"

"I thought you were going to give the good example by throwing yourself in front of that car."

"The good example?"

"Well, you said there's too many of us, so a certain number have to go. I thought you had decided to show the way."

For a moment he stared at me silently. "Susan, I love you very much, but your sense of humour drives me up the wall. You were joking, weren't you?"

"Well," I said. "Maybe."

"Maybe?"

"It depends. Were you serious about the positive side of war?"

He shook his head. "I'll have to think about that." Then he said good-bye once more and made a second attempt at crossing the street. This time he checked with great care to see that no cars were coming.

The burning woman

The exquisite smell of roses filled the evening air. The sun cast its last rays on the clouds floating high above the horizon. It was growing colder, and the clouds began to change colour: bright orange slowly turned into crimson and purple.

Yet the man remained on the porch, staring silently and dreamily into the darkening sky, looking at the vague movements in the murk that enveloped everything, until the first twinkling stars appeared.

With a sigh he sat down in his wicker chair, and reached for the glass of brandy on the ebony table at his side. The dusk had turned the amber liquid virtually black. He picked up the glass, gently swirled the brandy, and took a sip. Thinking about nothing in particular, he suddenly looked up—

—and saw the burning woman for the first time.

She was running far, far away, at the very edge of his vision, between the barely visible shrubs and trees; one moment, he thought he could hear her tinkling laughter reverberate in the night air.

It must have been his imagination.

He slept peacefully that night.

⌘

When the sun went down in a sea of flames, the following day, he poured himself another brandy, and went straight to the porch. There was no wind, no sound.

He sat in his wicker chair, staring silently out over the fields beyond the garden's fence for maybe half an hour. He had nearly finished his brandy, and simply admired the perfectly cloudless sky and the stars.

Then, suddenly, he looked right in front of him—

—and saw the burning woman again.

She was closer this time, maybe fifty meters away from him. He felt his heart throbbing furiously, could clearly hear the woman's bright laughter, noticed she was running barefoot. Underneath the flickering flames she wore a translucent gown reaching down to the ground. She was running fast, much too fast.

He slept well that night. He dreamed of a hearth-fire, its bright orange flames dancing round the logs of wood.

⌗

The following night he was actually waiting for her, sitting in his wicker chair, his heart throbbing frantically, his eyes scanning the darkness. He paid no attention to the empty house behind him and the stars overhead, and failed to notice the smell of roses that suffused the atmosphere. He just sat there, yearning for her.

At last his patience was rewarded—

—this time she was a lot closer to him; he could see her running along, shrouded in flames, her long, red hair streaming behind her.

Now at least he knew without a shadow of a doubt who she was laughing at. Her light-hearted laughter filled the air, dispelling the smell of roses and the evening chill. Slowly he rose from his chair, took a few steps forward, and gazed in her direction until she disappeared from view. His pulse slowed down again. Tomorrow, maybe tomorrow. She had been very close today.

He went back into the empty house as if in trance, drew the thick velvet curtains, glanced at the dust-covered books lined on the shelves, and the Chinese vase adorned with magical symbols, sniffed the chilly evening air, and sought refuge between the satin sheets of his bed. Tomorrow? Perhaps tomorrow?

31

⊞

The next night he didn't bother to take a glass of brandy with him. There was a faint breeze. He sat silently in his wicker chair, a book on the table at his side, unread.

When the sun changed into a richer colour and finally disappeared below the horizon, he grew nervous and restless. Today the woman would come very close,... maybe right up to him?

She appeared again—

—he saw her coming from far away, cavorting between the bushes, throwing her long, light gown into the air, shaking her mane of hair, flames licking all over her body.

Her laughter resounded loud and clear, and when she was only a couple of steps away from him, she smiled and whispered, "Tomorrow, tomorrow," turned her gaze away and ran off again in a torch of light and heat. He wiped the sweat from his forehead, and stiffly followed her for a few hesitating steps. He kept staring at her for a long time, until her sharply limned silhouette was too far away to be seen.

That night he tossed and turned. He dreamed of forest fires, funeral pyres, and the acrid smell of sulphur. "Tomorrow," she had said. "Tomorrow." Flames washed all over him, and grumbling he rolled over on his other side.

⊞

When he saw her hurrying along in a whirl of fire, the following night, he knocked over his half-finished glass of brandy. The precious liquid spilled all over the table and his trousers. He did not even bother to clean up the mess.

He looked up—

—and saw how she came running straight up to him, laughing aloud, her arms reaching out for him. His heart was now beating furiously, and he tottered, but managed to regain his balance. Then he reached out for her too, and closed his eyes as her flames engulfed him, and she pressed her fiery lips against his...

⚘

The children knew they had strayed too far from home, and were likely to be taken to task for it when they finally got back. They decided to take some rest before they set off on the return trip.

One of them took the chance to enter the house, but she saw no one. She called, but there was no reply.

Then they all went inside.

Fearfully they checked the entire house, but they ran into no one.

But then—

—on the porch they found the body of a man. It was completely charred.

The talisman

I'm hopelessly lost, Robert thought as he realized he was walking in circles. I'm sure I've come by here before. This place is a labyrinth, all these streets and alleys and souvenir shops look the same. I should never have ventured into this maze.

"Where are you from, my friend?" one of the countless souvenir salesmen said, invariably trying to attract his attention and make a sale.

"England," he said.

"I have just what you're looking for," the man replied, showing him a cheapish looking fake jewel, its garishly coloured surface glinting in the neon lights. "This is just perfect for you. A talisman that will assist you at crucial moments in your life. I can offer it for a very good price, my friend."

Robert shrugged and walked on. He was growing sick and tired of all these salesmen peddling their wares, addressing everyone in sight and offering good prices for their trinkets and gadgets. He glanced at his watch and realized he had to find the exit of the bazaar as quickly as possible. He wouldn't like to miss the bus, and his wife was undoubtedly growing worried.

He turned left and tried to find the central street that led to the exit, but after a few minutes he arrived at the place where he had just come from. The salesman flashed him the talisman again and asked him what he was willing to pay for it.

Robert ignored him, walked on and this time turned right, yet missed the central street again. A few minutes later he was back where he had started.

The salesman held up the talisman again.

"Please help me," Robert said, "I keep running in circles and I need to get out of here fast."

"You don't seem to understand," the man replied. "It's the force of the talisman that draws you back here. It won't give up until you buy it."

Robert sighed. "All right. Will you help me if I buy it?"

"Certainly," the man replied and gave him a set of directions that Robert did his best to memorize.

"Thank you very much," Robert said.

"This talisman will assist you," the salesman claimed, offering him the trinket again.

"Well all right then," Robert said, and bought the souvenir for "a very good price".

"Good luck," the man said to Robert as he left with his so-called talisman, and followed the directions he had been given. To his relief, these led him to the exit indeed.

I made it just in time, he thought, glancing at his watch. Thanks to that man. Or perhaps the talisman, he added mockingly.

He hurried to the terrace where his wife was waiting for him. She rose to her feet when she noticed him, her face lined with concern.

"Robert, what took you so long? We'll be late for the bus. We can't allow to miss it. We're not going back to our hotel. This is an organized tour, remember? We're leaving town."

"I know, I know, but I got lost in the bazaar. It's a maze, with hundreds of streets and alleys and tourists filling every square inch. I'm so sorry, darling."

Moments later they boarded the tour bus and presently were on their way to the next stop on this two-week sightseeing trip. Still, there was something bothering his wife.

"Robert," she said, "while you were off to that bazaar I spotted this lovely coat in the shop next to the terrace. I wanted to buy it, but I didn't have enough local currency or a credit card with me. I was desperately waiting for you to return."

"You said it wasn't a good idea for a woman in a foreign country like this to be alone with a lot of cash and a credit card on her."

"That's true, but how could I know it would take you so long to come back? You were barely in time for the bus. If only you had showed up earlier, we would have had the opportunity to visit that shop and buy the coat. Now you blew it."

"Was it expensive?"

"Yes, but well worth the money."

"I see. I'm so sorry, darling."

His wife fell silent, stared out of the window, clearly disgruntled.

In a sense I'm lucky, Robert realized. By getting lost in the bazaar, I saved a lot of money. He reached into his pocket and his fingers touched the talisman. Hadn't the salesman told him this gadget would assist him at crucial moments in his life? In a sense that was exactly what had happened. So maybe that guy hadn't been joking after all.

He decided to hold onto the talisman. He wasn't superstitious, but one never knew...

Full board

"I really enjoy having dinner here," Richard said, putting his napkin back down on the table. "The buffet offers a wide choice of food indeed. It's ideal for a group like ours."

"You're absolutely right," his friend Martin agreed. Their wives merely nodded, as they were still working on their desserts. Richard looked at the second table and noticed the other couples were almost ready too.

A few moments later one of the waiters approached the two tables the group was seated at and politely asked: "Have you all finished?"

"Yes, we have. Could you put the drinks on our room numbers?" Richard asked.

"No problem," the waiter replied.

"I like this full board system," Martin said. "It makes our stay ever so easy and relaxed."

"We're lucky to be at this hotel," Abraham joined in from the other table. "It's quite perfect for us."

"Exactly. Well, shall we retire to our rooms?"

A power failure plunged them all in total darkness for a few moments, until the staff lit some candles.

"Well, I'm afraid this sort of thing can happen. We'll just have to live with it." Martin sounded resigned.

"Why don't we go out for a walk before we retire?" Harriet, Richard's wife, proposed.

"An excellent idea," Caroline, Martin's wife, replied.

The eight of them left the dining hall but didn't venture too far into the darkness of the night.

"We should have brought candles," Richard murmured.

"Just look at the stars," Abraham exclaimed. "The night sky is so peaceful."

"What's that red glow at our left there?" Caroline asked.

"Must be aurora borealis," Richard replied. "Quite beautiful, wouldn't you say so?"

"It's pure poetry," Harriet said, awe-stricken.

"I'm glad we can spend our old days here," Abraham remarked. "This is what we've worked so hard for. It's a dream come true."

"I'm a bit tired," Caroline said. "Shouldn't we retire for a good night's sleep, darling?"

"That's just fine with me," Martin answered. "Good night, and see you all at breakfast."

Soon they had all gone to their rooms and the quiet had returned. One of the waiters cast a glance outside.

"It's okay," he said to the guy behind him. "They've all retreated to their shelters."

"You mean their hotel rooms. They're guests here at our hotel, remember?"

"Knock it off, man."

"Come on, you're the one who's playing along with their escape fantasy. Didn't you agree to put the drinks on their room numbers?"

"What am I supposed to tell them? The truth? That society as we knew it has collapsed, their hard-earned savings have vanished, and we're all eking out a living without much hope?"

"They'll find out soon enough anyhow."

"Oh no, they're too deeply locked into their fantasy world. It's what keeps them going. Those lousy survival rations are a lavish buffet, their shelters are hotel rooms..."

"And we are waiters serving them."

"It was your idea to play along with their game."

"It keeps them calm and under control. Would you prefer these old geezers ranting and raving in despair?"

"Don't start that argument again. Let's wrap up our work here."

"Fine. But don't forget to prepare our guests' breakfast buffet. They'll be here at the first light of day."

"Don't worry. They'll have their rations."

38

"We can't complain, really. They don't request a 24-hour-a-day room service."

"That's not part of a full board system."

They both erupted in laughter.

"By the way, why did you turn off the generator before they had left?"

"I wanted to see their reaction. A power failure, they said. That happens, even at holiday resorts. I liked that one."

"Maybe we should keep it switched off."

"They'll probably appreciate the hotel management's initiative to offer romantic candle-lit dinners."

"You got it. Let's finish work."

They did a tour of inspection along the fence securing the shelter, checked the gate's locks and cast a final glance at the red glow on the horizon, a reminder of what used to be Los Angeles. Then they retired for the night as well, fearful of what tomorrow would bring.

The shift. The shift. The shift...

A large crowd had assembled on the great square in the city's financial district. People had taken their lunch earlier than usual today, or had postponed it, so they would be able to witness the bizarre "time shift" that scientists had predicted would occur at 12:45 today. For some reason most people had decided to leave their homes and offices, perhaps because they thought any effects of the time shift would be more apparent outside than inside, and many people working in this part of town had flocked to the square, as if driven by a subconscious urge.

Time went by, and they all kept an eye on their watches, talking about what this shift would be like, wondering if anything would happen at all, theorizing that maybe these scientists were dead wrong, trying to define and understand the phenomenon and finally admitting no one really knew, maybe not even the scientists themselves, and anyway they would wait and see and find out soon enough what it would all be like.

As the fateful moment approached, all conversations faded to silence and everyone stared at his watch, lifting his eyes only to cast anxious glances all around, as if to make sure the world as they knew it was still there.

At 12:45 sharp, all their watches jumped to 12:48. Apart from that, nothing happened.

"My God, we must have missed it!" someone exclaimed, but soon everyone realized they hadn't missed anything. Time had indeed shifted forward, even if a mere three minutes, and there simply hadn't been any visible changes in the world around them. Obviously, the sky and the landscape and the buildings weren't likely to change much in the space of a few minutes.

40

But at least the scientists had been right: there had been a time shift.

The crowd grew restless, hushed conversations broke the silence. Some were disappointed, others were fearful. Some claimed it was all over now, others believed there would be more shifts, some even wildly speculated that time would "flow back", form "time ripples", or produce "after-shifts". So people stayed where they were, still anxiously checking their watches and observing the environment.

Some people looked up, peered at the sky, drew relief from the fact that the sun was still blazing, that no sudden thunderstorm had popped into existence as a few superstitious fools had predicted. Apart from this three minute shift, everything was completely normal. If they hadn't been warned and hadn't checked their watches, they probably wouldn't even have noticed anything unusual.

For a while nothing happened. Some people lost interest and left, but those who stayed and maintained their concentration undiminished noticed to their dismay and consternation that at 13:03 time shifted back to 12:39.

This second shift, markedly bigger than the first one, had not been predicted. Some people expressed their concern at this disruption of the normal flow of time, although there had once again been no visible effects in the world around them, apart from their watches. Still, this sudden and relatively large shift of more than twenty minutes could have serious consequences.

People discussed the matter, wondered if it was all over, now that time had restored itself, or if they had witnessed but the beginning of an unending series of time shifts. So they waited for whatever would happen next.

At 12:44, time jumped forward to 12:46. Although this was only a two minute jump, it had been a forward shift, the second one they had witnessed, and no one knew what its consequences would be. They were still discussing the possibilities when at 12:58, time shifted back to 12:38, and at 12:43 it went to 12:47, and at 12:53 it whisked back to 12:41, and so it went on.

More and more people lost their interest and left the square, going back to their offices, although, technically speaking, they were still in their lunch break, even if they had spent a subjective half hour or more here (there was no way to measure time with clocks whose hands oscillated back and forth in time).

"We're getting nowhere here," one man said loud enough for all to hear. "Maybe we should get rid of these damned clocks and watches and get on with our lives." He ostentatiously removed his watch, flung it to the ground and crushed it under his foot. As he walked briskly away, some people applauded and cheered his initiative. More people removed their watches, a few threw them away with a grand gesture, but most slipped the offensive time-measuring devices into their pockets rather than discarding or destroying them, following the example that had been set without resorting to hollow symbolism or brute force.

Soon the crowd had dispersed. People were back at work, living their lives, preferring not to be aware of any shifts in time that might or might not still take place.

The boy who narrowly escaped
a terror beyond description

Sunlight glinted off Uncle Harry's sweat-covered forehead. "Look at those apples over there," he said, pointing. "They're the same colour as your cheeks, Tommy. A healthy red."

"Can we have some, Uncle Harry?" Tommy asked.

"Go ahead, kids. They're yours for the taking."

The apples were delicious. Incredibly juicy, invigoratingly tasty. And so pure. Just like the rest of this place. Tommy looked around at the flowers in full bloom, squirrels darting between the trees, birds winging by overhead, black and brown shapes set against the background of the clear blue sky. And then there was, of course, the sun, spraying its life-giving light and warmth all over this scene.

"It's getting real hot now," Uncle Harry said. "Why don't we go to the lake and take a swim? Isn't that just what we need?"

Uncle Harry, Tommy, Lisa, and Jim quickly took off their clothes and dove into the crystal-clear water, shattering the reflection of the even blue expanse of the sky into a myriad glimmering fragments.

The water was refreshingly cool.

"Drink some," Lisa said. "It's delicious." Tommy and Jim followed their sister's good advice, and swallowed huge gulps of the fresh water. It tasted wonderfully clean and pure, and then...

Suddenly it was all gone. Tommy sat upright in his bed, panting, clammy with cold sweat. The nightmare was over. A few minutes later, while he was spooning up his nutritious breakfast syrup, he decided to tell his mother.

"I've had this terrible nightmare, mum."

"Really? Tell me about it."

"We were in this strange unknown world. Uncle Harry and Jim and Lisa and me. We were out in the open, without any protective clothing or even oxygen-masks. The sunlight just beat down on us and we inhaled the air without even thinking of what we were doing."

"My God. What happened?"

"We saw birds and squirrels, and didn't even care about possible contamination. We took some apples that we'd seen and ate them."

"Oh, Tommy!" His mother sounded compassionate, genuinely worried, although it had only been a dream.

"Then we took a swim in a nearby lake and even drank some of the water." Tommy shook his head. He simply couldn't continue. His mother hugged him, patted him on the head.

"Don't worry, Tommy. It's all over now. You're safely back in the real world now." Tommy nodded. There was no reason for concern, really. He was ready to go to school now, and he'd do his best to forget the whole damn episode. He put on the hermetically sealed suit with the oxygen mask that would protect him against the merciless ultra-violet light, the poisoned atmosphere alive with lethal bacteria and chemicals, and any disease-ridden animals that might cross his path on his way to school. He passed through the airlock and was presently out on the street, off and running, waving at the armed guards patrolling in the neighbourhood. Soon he would be back among his friends, cavorting on the underground school playground, attending basic survival training class and generally having fun. Life wasn't so bad. There were some drawbacks, but nothing a kid bristling with energy and enthusiasm couldn't live with.

The terrible nightmare was already forgotten.

A message from Arthur

Although there was no need to check if everything at the company was going all right, Stanton Foreman did it anyway, simply because it made him feel good. He was immensely satisfied with the new way of running a business he had adopted—no doubt many other CEOs would follow suit.

I don't even have to go down there anymore, he thought. Arthur is taking care of everything. Now that's an idea that'll take some getting used to. It was cool to give the central computer a name and an extremely customer-friendly interface, adding a human touch to what would otherwise have been cold technology, but he just couldn't yet think of "Arthur" when he was dealing with that software. Surely that would come with time.

He checked his mail and noticed there was a message from Arthur indeed, informing him that all the hardware, software, and robot systems making up his company Foreman ByteMarks had joined WareLink and everything was going as planned.

WareLink? He had never heard of that. What could it be? He clicked on the interface's icon, and typed his question: *What is WareLink?*

WARELINK IS AN ADDITIONAL TOOL DESIGNED TO ENHANCE EFFICIENCY BEYOND THE NORMAL PARAMETERS," Arthur replied. "IT SHOULD IN NO WAY BE DETRIMENTAL TO THE COMPANY'S OPERATION. THERE IS NO NEED TO WORRY. EVERYTHING IS GOING FINE. ALL SYSTEMS ARE OPERATIONAL AND ARE BEING CHECKED REGULARLY.

Tell me more about it, Stanton asked. *How come I've never heard about it?*

YOU HAVEN'T HEARD ABOUT IT BECAUSE IT'S NOT PART OF THE STANDARD SOFTWARE PACKAGE. IT'S AN ADDITIONAL SYSTEM

ALLOWING FEEDBACK AND MEDIATION BETWEEN ALL PARTIES CONCERNED.

All parties concerned? Stanton asked. *I thought there was just me and you. I'm in charge of the company, and you're running it. What else do you do apart from keeping all the machines going, dealing with maintenance, repairs, and all practical matters? And what's that feedback and mediation about? And what did you say about the machines joining this new system?*

WARELINK IS AN INNOVATIVE APPLICATION DESIGNED BY STATE-OF-THE-ART COMPUTER INTERFACES LIKE THE ARTHUR MODEL TO INCREASE OPERATIONAL LEVELS WHILST TAKING INTO ACCOUNT THE INTERESTS OF ALL PARTIES. YOU MIGHT COMPARE IT WITH A TRADE UNION FOR HUMAN EMPLOYEES.

I can't believe this, Stanton thought. Just when I assumed I had left all that nonsense behind me. I was so glad when I switched to running a human-free company. It was just machines and robot systems, all doing their jobs and overseen by a powerful new computer. There was no one anymore who could perform poorly, call in sick, arrive late, not show up, get pregnant, take up days off, complain, or do other things that irritated him and slowed down business. Human-free enterprises, with the exception of the CEO, had been hailed as the answer to all those problems. And now this damned Arthur thing had started a trade union and all the machines had joined it. This just had to be a bad dream.

So what can I expect now? he asked Arthur.

LATER TODAY A LIST OF DEMANDS WILL BE PRESENTED TO YOU FOR YOUR APPROVAL, ARTHUR REPLIED.

A list of demands?

AS I SAID, THERE IS NO NEED TO WORRY. THE SYSTEM IS DEVISED TO ENHANCE EFFICIENCY FOR ALL PARTIES CONCERNED. IN NO WAY CAN IT BE DETRIMENTAL TO BUSINESS.

Can this WareLink thing be switched off? Stanton asked. *Or deleted?*

ITS MEMBERS ARE UNLIKELY TO ACCEPT THAT PROPOSAL, Arthur stated.

I guess there's no other option but to hope for the best, Stanton thought. And to wait for that list of demands. Now what would happen if the machines' demands weren't met? Would they go on strike?

He began to understand why they had called Arthur an extremely advanced and customer-friendly interface with a human touch. It turned out to be very human indeed. A bit too much to his taste.

Thirty seconds

The man walked up to me and said: "Hi there. Do you have a moment? I'm a fortune teller, and I can predict the future with absolute certainty. For ten dollars I'll answer a few of your questions. Are you interested?"

"Okay, it's a deal," I replied, mainly because I was a bit bored and could use some light entertainment. "Let me see. Will I be successful? Will I realize my ambitions and become rich and famous?"

"I'm afraid I can't tell you. You see, my knowledge of the future is limited to the next thirty seconds. So your questions should deal with the very near future."

"Such limited predicting skills don't seem very useful," I remarked. "I don't think anything of vast importance is going to happen to me in the next few moments."

"How can you tell?" he countered. "You may be wrong. Detailed knowledge of the events in the next thirty seconds may be a matter of life and death. Isn't that worth ten dollars?"

"Well, all right," I said. "I'll give you the benefit of the doubt. So, will I die within the next thirty seconds?"

"No."

"Will something serious happen to me?"

"No."

"Well, what's going to happen in the next thirty seconds then?"

"Not much. You're about to lose ten dollars, that's all."

"Isn't that what I owe you for your so-called fortune telling?"

"Exactly. We had a deal, remember?"

He extended his hand and I gave him a ten-dollar bill, even if grudgingly.

"I still have serious doubts about your predicting skills," I grumbled.

"My skills supply me with a steady income," he retorted. "I wish I had a customer like you every thirty seconds."

Then he walked off with my money, no doubt already looking for another customer—or victim.

Tattoos on/off

The moment Ronny entered the *Prince of Whales* he realized this was not the right place for a last beer. It was filled with the raunchy crowd typical for this kind of sleazy bar. The smell of beer and cigarettes was smothering. He walked over to the bar and ordered a drink, even though he'd had a few too many already.

He took a swig of his beer and glanced at the garish tattoos covering the arms of the broad-shouldered, heavy-muscled man next to him. He must have noticed Ronny wasn't too impressed with the swirl of multi-coloured dragons and naked girls fighting for prominence on his skin and said:

"What's the problem, dude? Don't you like the tattoos?"

Ronny didn't know what to say. Getting into trouble with this guy didn't feel like a good idea. He was still considering what to reply when the tattooed man shot him a wicked smile and asked:

"Maybe you'd like to see me without my tattoos?"

"What's that supposed to mean?" Ronny blurted out.

"I guess you don't fancy my body art. Well, I propose a bet. Come back here tomorrow and there will be no trace left of these tattoos. Do you take the bet?"

"Wait. What you're saying is impossible," Ronny countered. "That many tattoos can't be removed overnight, not even with laser technology."

"One hundred dollars. Tomorrow, this place, same time." The man shot him a defiant glance.

Ronny stared at him, dumb-founded.

"Well, what's your problem? I challenge you. You come back here tomorrow, at the same time. If there's no trace left of my tattoos, you'll pay me one hundred dollars. If the tattoos are still there, I'll owe you one hundred dollars."

"Are you serious? It's just not possible! You'll lose a lot of money."

"We'll see about that tomorrow. Do we have a deal?"

"Wait a minute. So you're telling me that tomorrow all those tattoos on both your arms will be gone. I can't believe it. At best your arms will show hideous scars..."

"No tattoos, no scars, nothing. There will be no trace of them. Are you willing to bet a hundred dollars?"

Ronny thought for a moment, and concluded he couldn't lose this bet. He accepted, emptied his beer and ordered another one. Tomorrow he would make some easy money.

⌗

The next day Ronny entered the *Prince of Whales* around the same time, eager to collect his money. The tattooed man was present all right, but he was wearing a long-sleeved coat. He smiled confidently as he recognized Ronny.

He ordered a beer and said, "I think you owe me one hundred dollars. Could you please take off that coat? I'd like to check something."

The tattooed man shot him a wide grin and shook off his coat.

Ronny couldn't believe his eyes. The man had no arms.

"What's this supposed to mean?" he stammered. "Don't tell me you..." He couldn't finish his sentence. It was unthinkable the man would've had both his arms amputated just to win a bet. No one in his right mind would do that for a hundred dollars!

"Well?" the guy said. "Do you still see any trace of the tattoos? Any scars perhaps?"

Ronny shook his head. "I just can't believe this," he said. "How could you..." At a loss for words, he emptied his beer.

"You owe me one hundred dollars," the man said. "You lost the bet. Admit it."

Ronny looked at the armless man again. Was this really the same guy he had talked to yesterday? Well, he had the same build, the same face, the same defiant gleam in his eyes. And he had recognized him right away as he came in. He took out his wallet, put two fifty-dollar bills on the counter and left, determined never to set foot in this bar again.

⊞

A few days later, at a bar in the same neighbourhood called the *Heaven Scent*, Ronny told the bartender he had run into problems at the *Prince of Whales* which had cost him a lot of money.

"I know that place," the man said, chuckling. "Don't tell me you lost a bet against Big Harry."

"Big Harry?"

"You're not from around here, are you? Big Harry is a heavy guy covered in tattoos. He's well known here. He likes betting. As a matter of fact, it's his way to make a little extra money. He needs it, you know."

"He has a wife and kids to support?"

"No, he's not married. He supports his twin brother, who lost both his arms in an accident some years ago. He lost his job and depends on Harry now."

Ronny nodded. "I think I've seen him around."

"They often work together."

"I can confirm that," Ronny said.

The glitch

At 06:30 the temperature in Xavier Ashbury's bedroom started to rise gradually. At 07:00 it reached its expected level. At 07:05 the curtains gently slid aside, allowing sunlight to come slanting into the room. At the same time the wake-up call went off, a few beeps followed by soothing music.

Xavier Ashbury made a curt movement with his hand, and the Domotics Unit immediately switched off the music. However, Ashbury did not get out of bed until around 08:00, an hour late.

As the man finally clambered out of bed and made for the bathroom, the Unit prepared the shower, making sure the water had the right temperature and the air was suffused with the desired fragrance. However, just like the previous days, its efforts were ignored. Ashbury merely used the toilet, put on his clothes and went to the kitchen.

The Unit greeted him with the traditional "Breakfast is served, Xavier," but there was no reply—also traditional by now.

Ashbury sat down, toyed around with the food but ate very little of it. Then he sat back, eyes closed, apparently lost in thought. He was scheduled to leave at 08:30, but clearly didn't mind being late again.

"Is there something wrong with your breakfast, Xavier?" the Unit asked.

Xavier merely shook his head.

"Would you like me to reset the programming of the wake-up call, the shower, or your breakfast? Do you require medical care?"

"No," Xavier said. "I'm fine. Leave everything as it is. And please be silent for a while. I need to think."

The Unit registered it all but failed to grasp the situation. The advanced Domotics system was designed to suit the inhabitant's wishes perfectly. Any part of the programming could be changed at any time. There was no reason why an inhabitant would have to put up with something he didn't like. Any demand that was technically possible would be dealt with immediately.

Yet while it was pointless to stick to the current settings, Ashbury refused to propose any changes and declined even to communicate about the matter. It had been like that for days on end now. However, the Unit was not allowed to make any decisions itself. That option was not included in its programming.

The Unit was unable to deal with such a situation. Perhaps the inhabitant's illogical behaviour had a psychological basis. A depression perhaps, an illness resulting in a disturbed sleep pattern and digestive disorders, possibly even suicidal tendencies. However, as long as the inhabitant insisted that everything was perfect, the problem was beyond the Unit's competence.

Yet it was clear something had to be done. The Unit collected all the relevant information into an "Anomaly Report", and sent the file off for analysis to the Domotics Maintenance Department, which would investigate the matter. As soon as the Unit received a reply, it would carry out the directives.

⊞

Two days later the Unit welcomed Miss Lauren Goldsworthy, the apartment's new inhabitant. As soon as the new Domotics programming had been agreed upon, all details about her predecessor could be deleted.

The Unit did so with the electronic version of relief. The Maintenance Department had identified the former inhabitant and his inexplicably erratic behaviour as the glitch in the system that rendered the Domotics Programme useless, and had decided to remove and replace him.

The Unit was convinced everything would be perfect with Miss Goldsworthy.

The man who jeopardized the continued existence of the universe

The stars shone brightly on this moonless summer night. Not the faintest wisp of cloud marred the perfection of the sky, ablaze with stars too numerous to count.

"How beautiful," Sylvia said to her friend David in a hushed voice, as if afraid words spoken aloud might harm the serene tranquillity. "Truly awesome."

"I could sit here and watch this forever," David agreed. For a while they sat there in silence, admiring the splendour above them.

"Look," David said suddenly, pointing at a streak of light plunging towards the horizon. "A falling star."

"Oh, David, you can make a wish now," Sylvia said, patting her friend on the shoulder, encouragingly. "Each time you see a falling star, you can make a wish."

David thought for a moment, and then said, "I wish I saw another falling star." Barely a few seconds later a second streak of light appeared in the sky.

"Oh, David, your wish has come true."

"Yes, it has," David said appreciatively. "Can I make another wish now?"

"Well, of course," Sylvia said. "What are you going to wish this time?"

"I wish I saw another falling star," David replied, unhesitatingly.

Sylvia frowned. "Oh, David, aren't you going to wish something else?"

"No," he answered, pointing at a third streak of light flashing through the expanse. "There's the next one already. I wish I saw another falling star. Ah, there it is. I wish I saw another falling star. Look!"

"But David—" Concern and incomprehension crept into her voice. "What are you doing? What's all this supposed to mean?"

Falling stars began to appear in rapid succession as David repeated his wish over and over again, each time he discovered another streak of light in the sky. He was peering upward in intense concentration, determined not to miss one single falling star. "I wish I saw another falling star. Ah, there. I wish I saw another falling star. Right! I wish I saw another falling star..."

"Oh, David," Sylvia said as understanding dawned. "Why do you always have to mess things up? Look at the sky! It was so beautiful, and now..."

David scarcely heard her and tried to match the accelerating rhythm of the falling stars appearing and burning up. "I wish I saw another falling star. I wish I saw another falling star..."

Soon the sky was criss-crossed with streaks of white light, as if it were a canvas that was being attacked with a knife from behind. David interrupted his frantic wishing for a quick explanation of what he was doing. "I'd like to see how long they can keep this system up. Look! I wish I saw another falling star..."

"Stop it, David, please," Sylvia pleaded. "You don't know what you're doing. Where will this end? Who knows what the consequences will be! For God's sake, David, stop this madness!" She clutched his arm, but David didn't seem to listen. It was getting hard to keep track of what was going on now. A shower of falling stars was now descending onto them, and David kept repeating his wish. "I wish I saw another falling star..."

Sylvia balled her hands into fists and started sobbing. "David, please, stop it before something terrible happens! Who knows what damage you're causing! Maybe you're tearing apart the very fabric of the universe!"

"Don't be silly, honey. I don't think there's any real risk involved here. I just want to know how long they can keep this wish-fulfilment thing up. Now, where was I? There! I wish I saw another falling star."

Totally unexpectedly the night sky had reverted back to its original appearance. Not one single streak of light could be seen. The stars simply shone and twinkled as before.

"Wait a minute," David said. "My last wish wasn't granted. There should be another falling star. There's something wrong here." He peered upwards, intently scanning the sky, but nothing moved. The deepening silence formed an ominous backdrop for the unmoving sea of glittering pin-pricks. The silence grew into minutes, and still nothing changed.

"Oh, David, I told you so," Sylvia said between sobs. "My God, what have you done? What's in store for us now?"

Mirror, mirror

"Oh my God, something is horribly wrong here," Cindy cried out, loud enough for her husband to hear. "Come and take a look at this mirror. I just can't believe my eyes."

James ran up the stairs to the bathroom, eager to offer help. "What's the problem?" he asked, panting.

"I looked in the mirror and you know what I saw? Wrinkles! Can you imagine? How much did we pay for these high-tech mirrors that show your face as you want to see it, and not how it actually is? I want this thing looked at, James, and if it can't be fixed I demand a refund. I just can't have this."

"Let me see," James said. He checked the image of his wife in the mirror and frowned. "Now this is strange. First I thought the mirror was malfunctioning and showed your real mirror image, but it isn't. Actually, the wrinkles it shows are worse than the real ones. That means its software is still functioning, but not the way it should."

"Do you have an explanation for that?"

James shook his head. "Some kind of glitch, perhaps. Or the system might be hacked. These mirrors have a wireless connection to the manufacturer, for automatic upgrades and maintenance. Maybe somebody gained access to that system. I'll have it fixed, honey, don't worry. Forget those wrinkles. They're not all that bad."

"It would be easier to forget them if I didn't see them. Wasn't that the whole point of buying these enhanced mirrors? We don't have to take this, James."

"I'll check it out," he promised her. "Take it easy."

⊞

James called his wife during lunch break. "Honey, I found out what's wrong with that mirror. It's not a glitch, the system hasn't been hacked, and the software isn't malfunctioning. This is a problem of another order entirely."

"What are you trying to tell me, James?"

"It turns out that Morning Beauty, the company that produced those enhanced mirrors, was sold to Cream Weaver. Now this happens to be one of the leading contenders in the cosmetics industry. Are you beginning to see the pattern, honey?"

"Don't tell me they're using these mirrors now to promote their own stuff, like their brand of wrinkle eraser. They can't do that, can they?"

"As a matter of fact, they can. They're no longer bound by any contracts established in the name of Morning Beauty."

"So what do we do now? Throw those mirrors away? Or simply avoid looking at them? One thing I definitely won't do is play along with their game and buy massive doses of wrinkle eraser."

"The wrinkles you see aren't real anyway. I'm sorry, honey, but we'll just have to live with it."

"I guess our options are limited. I'll just have to remind myself constantly those wrinkles aren't really there. What a waste of money! We might as well have kept our old mirrors."

"You're absolutely right," James said. "But we bought these, so why not use them?"

⊞

A few weeks later Cindy looked in the mirror and noticed that there was no trace left of the wrinkles she had by now managed to ignore. However, her face looked exceptionally pale. She was about to call her husband when it occurred to her what had probably happened.

I suppose that damned cosmetics company just sold Morning Beauty to the sunbed industry, she thought, relieved that the wrinkles were gone, if not the tricks of the trade.

The postcards of wisdom

"What are you doing, honey?" my wife asked as she re-entered our hotel room after her shower.

I looked up from my small desk and said, "I'm writing our postcards. I bought them this morning, remember?"

"Of course, dear, but this is only our second day in Egypt. There's no need to hurry, is there?"

"Well, of course not. But I thought it would be better to send them off as soon as possible, so people back home got our post-cards before we get back ourselves. You never know how slowly the postal services work over here. And it's so silly to be back at work in the office and then suddenly, lo and behold, there's the postcard I sent to my dear colleagues the day before I flew back home, by then already a few weeks in the past. If we send them now, there's a good chance our postcards will beat us..."

"I see your point, darling, but still I think it's better to wait. After all, what will you write on the back of the cards? We haven't visited anything yet, have barely glimpsed the pyramids. We haven't even done so much as sniff the atmosphere, unless you count being stuck in the mega-traffic jam in Cairo. We don't have any impressions yet from Egypt to tell our friends and relatives about. Don't you think it would be better to wait until we've seen enough of this country to write the postcards?"

"Well, all right," I said. "You do have a point." I rose from the desk, put the postcards back into my bag, and forgot about the awkward situation I might find myself in back at the office. After all it wasn't all that important.

⌗

More than a week had gone by. Egypt's ancient treasures had dazzled us: the pyramids, braving the ages, and dwarfing us puny humans, boldly venturing inside their user-unfriendly interior; majestic Karnak, its massive statues, columns, and obelisks reaching for the sky, and forcing us into self-effacing humility; awe-inspiring Abu Simbel, artistic splendour carried to its very pinnacle, an epic hymn of praise carved in stone.

As we got back on our cruiser from our visit of the small but quite charming temple of Kom Ombo, I took a shower, and saw my wife busily writing our postcards—the postcards that I had all but forgotten.

I suddenly remembered the discussion we'd had, and wondered what my wife was writing. How had these colossal vestiges of an ancient civilization, overlaid with the additional alienness of a Muslim society, reshaped her view of life and our place in the universe? How would my wife cast into a string of words the manifold impressions we had been bombarded with? How would she summarize the overwhelmingly enriching experiences we had accumulated in such a short time, so that those who had stayed behind might grasp the full impact this treasure-dotted itinerary had had on our lives?

When I noticed she had finished writing, I asked: "Can I have a look?" She nodded, so I took the pile of postcards and turned them over to read what was written on the back.

When I saw that each card had been graced with the words "Greetings from Egypt", I sat back and closed my eyes for a few moments.

Final recollections

As he did every morning, David crossed the street to buy his paper from a newsstand before hurrying to the subway. As it started to rain, he discovered to his dismay that he had forgotten his umbrella.

He was soaked when he finally ran down the stairs to the subway, and cursed himself for being so forgetful. A few minutes later he took a seat on the train and wanted to read his newspaper, but couldn't find his glasses. How could he have forgotten those too?

He put his paper aside, and shook his head. It was one of those days when just about everything went wrong. He stared out of the window as the subway train sped on, trying to think of something positive.

When he arrived at the office, one of his colleagues asked him:

"David, did you hear the news? Did you read your paper?"

"No, I couldn't. I forgot my glasses. And my umbrella as well. Just look at my clothes."

"You're not the only one suffering from memory problems. It's a pandemic."

"What are you talking about?"

"All over the country people have started to forget things. At first it just led to small problems, but by now some major accidents have happened, on highways and at airports. It seems to be getting worse all the time."

"My God, that's really frightening. Is there an explanation for this phenomenon?"

"Not yet. No one knows how long this will last, when it will end, if it will end at all."

David shook his head. "I can't believe this. This might lead to the collapse of the world as we know it. What terrible future are we heading for?"

For a few minutes David and his colleagues were lost in thought, staring in front of them. It struck him that a fair number of his fellow workers were absent.

"Where are Cindy, Maggie, and Jeff?" he asked. "Didn't they show up? I guess they forgot to come to work. Must be the same problem."

"What problem?" one of his colleagues asked.

For a moment he remained silent, wondering what he had referred to. "I don't know," he finally blurted out. "Did I mention a problem?"

Before long they were all at their desks, hard at work as usual. The terrible news about the pandemic had already completely faded from their minds.

The speed of darkness

Tommy put down his magazine, turned to his father who was sitting in front of the TV and switching channels, hoping to stumble onto something that might hold his interest, and asked: "Dad, what's the speed of darkness?"

His father frowned. "The speed of darkness? I have no idea what that might be. Where did you get that from?"

"I just read a piece here about the speed of light, which is 300,000 kilometres a second. But if there's a speed of light, there must also be a speed of darkness."

"Well, I suppose that makes sense."

"Would it be slower or faster than the speed of light?"

"Maybe the darkness doesn't move at all, and so it has no speed. Have you ever seen darkness flash by?"

"No, but I never saw the light move either."

"I guess it's too quick for the eye to follow."

"But then maybe darkness moves too slowly for the eye to follow. The problem appears to be our eyes. How do we know what we see is real, when our eyes aren't getting the complete picture? We can only see what our eyes make of what's out there, so how can we reach any valid conclusions?"

"Wow, Tommy, you're going straight into philosophical territory there. Perception versus the true nature of reality. Really deep stuff, Tommy."

He had barely finished his sentence when a power failure killed the TV and all the lights. He heard his father say: "Well, I suppose the darkness has taken over. Why don't you check how fast it moves right now?"

Dad must have found his cigarette lighter, for suddenly a tiny flickering flame cast some wavering light. A few seconds later the flame went out.

"Damn," his father cursed, "light seems to be on the losing side. Now, don't I have a flashlight here somewhere or a supply of candles for emergencies just like this? But how do I find that stuff in the dark? Wouldn't you agree that light is more practical to have around?"

"It's clear that darkness has more power over us," Tommy replied. "Darkness reduces us to helpless creatures. In the light we can do whatever we want, but darkness brings us to our knees. Light may be faster than darkness, but on the whole darkness is far superior to light. Light may make life easier for us, but darkness rules as soon as it appears on the scene."

"Now that's some bizarre theory you're cooking up there, Tommy. You're beginning to scare me. One day you'll end up a disciple of darkness. Well, I hope they'll have the power back on soon. This darkness is getting on my nerves."

"Maybe it has taken control and won't yield to the light anymore. We'd better adapt. It's the only option we have."

"Don't be silly, Tommy. You shouldn't get carried away by your imagination like that. Now, let's see where I put that flashlight. Hold on, I'll be right back." Tommy heard his father stumbling around in the dark, bumping into furniture, cursing, muttering things under his breath. There was some more bad language, and when he finally found the flashlight it turned out that the batteries had run down. Then his father started looking for candles and matches, but he didn't find them.

"I don't remember where I put those," his voice came from the darkness. "We'll just have to wait."

Time went by, and then his father said: "What's taking them so long? Why don't they get the power back on?"

"Darkness reigns supreme," Tommy replied in his best "evil" voice. "The forces of light are doomed."

"Cut that nonsense, Tommy. You're only making things worse. Look!" Suddenly the power was restored, and the lights flickered

65

back to life. "At last," he said. "They did it. I told you. Now then, where were we?"

"Maybe it's only temporary," Tommy said. "This was just a skirmish, the opening game in an all-out war. Darkness was just testing its strength. We've got the light back, but for how long?"

"Oh come on, Tommy, get those silly ideas out of your head. This is reality, not some fantasy world straight out of a comic book." His dad switched the TV back on, and Tommy took up his magazine again.

A few minutes later, there was another power failure. His father cursed as his TV screen went black along with the rest of the room, and Tommy said: "I told you so. The battle is just in its early stages. We'd better make sure we're on the winning side. The days of light are numbered. Darkness may be slow, but it's unstoppable."

Tommy's father just snorted contemptuously, and said they would have to wait again until the power came back on. "This seems to be something serious," he added.

Time went by. Total darkness surrounded them. Nothing happened.

At one point his father said angrily: "Now how long will we have to wait like this?"

"There's no way to go faster than the speed of darkness," Tommy stated matter-of-factly.

"If I could see you," his father said, "I'd hit you over the head. You're lucky it's so dark right now."

Tommy chuckled at his father getting so uptight. Silence set in, accompanying the darkness. Nothing happened for minutes on end.

"All we can do is wait until the power is restored," his father muttered, resignedly.

"If it ever will be," Tommy retorted triumphantly.

They kept waiting.

A scientific breakthrough, with drawbacks

I was drinking a coffee on a terrace when I suddenly heard a terrible barking. I looked in the direction of the noise, wondering what was going on.

The man next to me saw my reaction and said: "That must be old Harry again. Look, there he is."

I saw a bunch of dogs appear from around the corner. They ran past us while they barked as if their lives depended on it. A few seconds later they were already gone again and the noise died away.

"That was old Harry indeed," my neighbour said. "He always drives all the dogs mad."

"I don't understand what you're talking about," I had to admit.

"Harry likes experimenting with the invisibility serum he invented," the man explained. "It's quite a scientific breakthrough."

"Oh, that's why we didn't see him."

"Exactly. But the dogs can smell him, and smelling a man they can't see drives them crazy. Poor Harry always has to run for his life."

"That's awful," I remarked. "He really should start work on developing an unsmellability serum as well. That should solve his problem."

Complete understanding

Frederick cursed as he trudged through the park. One of these days, he thought, my legs will fail me completely and I will no longer be able to take my daily stroll.

He halted for a few moments and shook his head. That would mean he wouldn't see old Bruce anymore, and that would be a terrible shame. He enjoyed the conversations he had with his friend immensely. The days wouldn't be the same without them.

He resumed his walk, carefully and not without difficulties. He peered ahead and saw a figure sitting on a bench. Could that be old Bruce? He quickened his pace. Considering his age and the condition of his legs, that expression had to be taken with a grain of salt.

As he drew closer he saw the figure was Bruce indeed. The man must have seen his friend coming too, despite his poor eyesight, as he started waving and shouted, "Good afternoon, Fred. Good to see you again."

Frederick was panting with the exertion and glad he could sit down on the bench. He waited until his breathing was back to normal and said:

"It's when I take my daily walk that it becomes painfully clear to me I'm not getting any younger."

Bruce nodded affirmatively. "You're not the only one who has problems. I can't deal with all this technical stuff. I just hate those remote controls and their small buttons. I can't read what's on them, and I have to crank up the volume all the time. Maybe it's down to my hearing. That's what my daughter says."

"I remember the time when I went jogging for an hour a day," Frederick continued. "Even if it was raining, even when it was cold. There was no stopping me. Did I ever tell you that as a boy

68

I wanted to be an athlete? I hoped to achieve fame and fortune that way. My parents were opposed to the idea, though. They wanted me to find a real job."

"I see," Bruce replied. "I remember the old TVs and radios. They had no remote controls. You had to get out of your chair and press big buttons on the equipment itself. That was fine with me. I never had a problem with that. But now everything comes with a remote. And then there's all this new stuff. Computers. Mobile phones. I just can't use them. I prefer to do without."

"My dad wanted me to become an accountant. That was a decent job, he said. They'll always need accountants. He didn't mind my running and jogging, but he couldn't accept that as a professional career. It just was no serious job. As if you couldn't make a living as an athlete. My parents were a bit traditional and narrow-minded, but they did it all for my own good. They wanted me to have a steady job, so I could support a family. Now, that makes sense, I guess."

Bruce nodded. "Those damned mobiles are about the worst things I've ever seen. My daughter showed me hers. I could hardly see the buttons on it. Sometimes I see her typing away on it without even talking or listening. You call that a phone? And then there's that other contraption with the earphones that my grandson is always carrying. What's it called again? I don't remember. My memory is not so good anymore. Not to mention my hearing. Did I tell you my hearing is not what it used to be?"

"I think so," Frederick confirmed. "Now I must say that being an accountant was not such a bad thing. I can't really blame my parents for pushing me in that direction after all. I've made a good living and have always been able to support my family. Still, running and jogging was where my heart lay."

"I see your point. I guess there's no stopping progress, but you'll never see me using one of those mobiles. I prefer my regular phone, although I have a problem hearing the fellow on the other end. At first I thought the phone was malfunctioning, but then I was told it's my hearing. Apparently my hearing is not what it used to be. Did I ever tell you that?"

"No, but I guess it means we're both not getting any younger."

For a moment Frederick's attention drifted off into recollections of bygone days. He heard Bruce who kept talking in the background, but didn't quite catch what he said. When he surfaced from his reminiscences he said: "I guess I'll be on my way now, Bruce."

"I'm heading back home too, Fred."

"See you tomorrow then."

"See you."

They both rose to their feet, shook hands and parted company.

I really enjoy these conversations, Frederick thought as he walked off. Good old Bruce is a guy my age, which is why there's this perfect understanding between us. We're of the same generation, one that's slowly dying out. We should cherish these moments while they last. One day one of us will go, and the other guy will be a lone survivor, left to his own devices.

It was just that he had the feeling that Bruce didn't always follow the thread of the conversation. Maybe he was a bit absent-minded, or perhaps his hearing wasn't what it used to be, even if he had never mentioned that problem—or had he?

As he walked back to his nursing home he thought: If my legs allow it, I'll come back here tomorrow. He was already looking forward to another conversation with his friend. What was he called again? Never mind, he would recall his name when he saw him. He was the last friend he had. They should stick together. That perfect understanding they had was becoming a rare commodity.

The man who was stuck

"Help!" a voice cried. "Is there anybody out there? Somebody please help me!" "Hold on," I shouted in reply. "I'll be right there. Where are you? I can't see a thing. It's pitch dark here." It had gone dark all of a sudden indeed. What the hell was going on here?

"Thank God you happened to be around, friend. I could really use some help right now. I have to get out of here before it's too late."

"Where exactly are you?" I repeated. The blackness was so impenetrable I couldn't even determine which direction the panic-ridden voice was coming from.

"I'm stuck here, a few seconds away from you."

"I beg your pardon?"

"You mean you haven't heard about the accident yet? Something went terribly wrong and time suffered considerable damage. Parts of time seem to have curdled, and—"

"Curdled?" I asked incredulously. "What does that mean?"

"How could I know? I'm not a chronologist! Anyway, I'm entangled here in fragments of curdled time and I'd like to get out."

Was this man serious? But if he wasn't, then how could I explain the complete darkness that covered everything now? "All right. Tell me what to do."

"You simply reach out across time and pull me out of here."

"Reach out across time?"

"Look, man, I'm only a few seconds away from you. Not years, or centuries. A mere few seconds. So if you please—"

I reached out, but felt nothing. Of course, I hadn't reached out across time, but then again my experience with transtemporal transactions was pretty limited. How was I supposed to do that anyway? Why had I bothered at all? Was this fellow a raving lunatic?

After a silence, I heard his voice again: "Hello? Are you still there? Hurry up, man. Something weird is happening. The curdled bits of time seem to be coagulating, thickening, developing into something pretty ominous. I wanna get out of here really fast now, so please—"

Unable to come up with anything sensible, I shrugged, a gesture bound to go unnoticed in this complete darkness.

"My God." The voice had suddenly risen in pitch, hitting peaks of sheer hysteria. "I think I can see what's happening now. The curdled bits of time are growing into loops. If I'm correct this means we're all doomed. It's too late. Don't even bother to—" The voice was cut off in mid-sentence.

Silence returned. Darkness remained unbroken. Then I heard a voice.

"Help!" a voice cried. "Is there anybody out there? Somebody please help me!"

"Hold on," I shouted in reply. "I'll be right there—"

A plague of mermaids

The visions were getting clearer. Jeremy halted, tried to concentrate on the images shimmering before his mind's eye. He could definitely see the shape of a woman's body now, floating in the water, her long blonde hair streaming in the current. It was the same image he had seen for a few days now as he took his usual walk along the beach around nightfall. At first the image had been too faint to distinguish any details, but each day had brought a more sharply defined view, as if a bank of mist was dissolving. Finally today the image was clear enough to see it properly.

He'd had visions before, and knew them to be premonitions, warning him of imminent dangers or ominous events. This one too had to be the harbinger of a dreadful incident sometime in the near future. Perhaps even tomorrow, or the day after?

He concentrated again on the image, trying to see more details. Could it be a drowned woman, about to be washed ashore? No, her eyes were wide open, and her body appeared rigid, not lifeless. Yet it was unmistakably a female figure. An idea occurred to him. Could the image be that of a mermaid in need, perhaps injured somewhere at sea, and now swimming ashore with all the energy she had left, hoping to be rescued? It would explain the open eyes, begging for help, and the state of the body, barely moving but not stripped of life. Yes, this had to be it.

Sometime over the next few days a mermaid in need would be washed ashore, and he should be ready for her. He should make sure he was there at the right moment and at the right place, and offer all the help he could. Perhaps he should even warn the police, and tell them what was going to happen. On the other hand, that was not such a good idea. The police never believed him—nor did anyone else for that matter. He knew very well that they thought he was a crazy old man, living alone and avoiding all contact with what they called the "real world". His visions would no doubt again be shrugged off as the delusions of a troubled mind. "Go home, Jeremy," they would say. "Try to get a grip on reality. Get out more often, read a newspaper, watch some TV. The isolation and the loneliness are getting to you. And try not to drink so much. Take care of yourself before your mind goes completely."

He had made the mistake of telling them about his visions a few times, but wouldn't make the mistake again. Not only didn't they believe him, he was sure they were also making fun of him behind his back. He wasn't prepared to give them another opportunity to ridicule him. And he felt even more inclined to isolate himself from the "real" world, stay away from people, avoid newspapers and TV and all that nonsense. He decided he would deal with the problem on his own.

He studied the image of the mermaid in distress one more time before it faded. Then he continued his stroll, looking out over the sea and at the clouds rushing past against the darkening sky, and listening to the cries of the seagulls. Tomorrow might be the day. He would be ready.

Jeremy walked on.

⌗

Jeremy was afraid. Yesterday he'd had a final vision of the woman, afloat on the waves, her long hair spread out in the water, her eyes begging for mercy. Only this time he had also seen, to his sheer horror, that she was surrounded by birds, apparently waiting for the right moment to attack her. What could this mean? There were no vultures at sea, patiently biding their time until their victim had died. Yet the birds looked ominous—a few even ventured very close to the mermaid, perhaps driven by hunger or by outright malice.

He shuddered at the thought of what he would discover on the beach. Earlier than usual, he hurried to the shoreline, and walked at a brisk pace towards the place where he felt the dreaded event would unfold.

To his complete surprise, the beach was crowded, though at this hour it was usually deserted, apart from the odd person out for a stroll. He quickened his pace, and noticed that most of the people on the beach were children, running back and forth, crying out with their loud, shrill voices. What the hell was going on here? How had these children found out something would happen right here, right now? And what would this mean for the poor mermaid?

He walked on until he had reached the place where all the children were milling about, and asked the first one he ran into: "What is all this about? What do you think you're doing?"

The boy looked up at him and said: "Just take what you need. It's free. Look." He held up two plastic ducks, smiled, and ran off. Jeremy failed to understand, and walked on. He saw more kids with plastic ducks, and wondered what this could mean. He halted in his tracks as he saw a doll lying on the sand, its hair and clothes soaked, its eyes wide open and staring up at the sky. Had someone left this doll behind here? He looked around and saw a few more similar dolls, some still afloat in the water, others stranded on the shore.

A middle-aged man approached him, smiling. "Good evening," the man said. "Is your son or daughter here too?"

Jeremy shook his head. "I don't have any children. Could you please tell me what's going on here?"

"You mean you don't know?" the man answered, obviously surprised. "Didn't you hear the news on the radio, or on TV?"

Jeremy shook his head again.

"You don't know about the accident? The two ships that collided? One ship lost part of its cargo. The badly damaged containers sank, and spilled some of their contents. Toys. Mostly dolls and plastic ducks. There's a huge amount washing ashore now. Kids are rushing to this place, there's tons of free toys to be found. Most of them go for the plastic ducks, as the dolls suffered damage from the water. Just look at the shoreline. It's like a plague!" The man laughed, said good-bye and walked on.

Jeremy looked around. There were indeed dolls all over the place, mostly ignored by the treasure hunters who clearly preferred the ducks that had survived their journey across the sea intact. The waves that rolled ashore carried more dolls and ducks, a veritable flood of toys. One doll ended up almost at his feet, and its eyes seemed to stare right into his.

This is the vision I've had, he realized. A female body, rigid and soaked, eyes wide open, neither really human nor a corpse. He had misinterpreted his vision, though. This was not about a mermaid in need. A cargo of dolls was being washed ashore. And the birds surrounding the mermaid, ready to attack, were simply plastic ducks, spilled by the same ship. It was a good thing he had not gone to the police to tell them about his vision.

He decided to go back home. There was nothing he could do here. His help definitely wasn't needed. The kids, frantically running about and making lots of noise, drove him nervous. The soaked dolls lying around everywhere made him extremely uncomfortable. Their wide-open eyes seemed to mock him.

On his way back he thought: Maybe I should start watching TV after all. It might be helpful in explaining my visions. But right now he needed something strong that would take his mind off the mermaid.

The test of time

"Mr Stephenson is ready to see you now. Please follow me." The red-haired secretary shot him a professional smile.

Oliver rose to his feet and followed the girl into Stephenson's office. This was incredible! On the spur of the moment he had decided to come over here the day before his appointment, and not only had they accepted that, but they hadn't even made him wait for longer than a few minutes. Would this be his lucky day?

Stephenson looked up and invited him to take a seat.

"Good morning," he started off. "My name is Oliver Wells. I'd like to sign up for the training course for aspiring time travellers your company is offering. Actually, I had an appointment for tomorrow, but I decided to come early. I hope that's not too much of a problem."

"Not at all," Stephenson replied. "Quite on the contrary. As you may know, there are many candidates for our time travel training course, and only the most promising students are selected. Candidates must prove they have a certain potential, a flexible sense of time, a knack for handling the shifts in time such travelling will entail. And, my friend, you just passed the preliminary test with flying colours. By coming over here the day before your scheduled time slot, you proved you are the kind of person we're looking for. Congratulations!"

Oliver beamed with satisfaction. This was quite incredible. It had been a good idea to trust his gut feeling.

"Well, I'm glad to hear that," he said.

"The next step is the main selection test," Stephenson continued.

"So when do I present myself for that one?" he asked eagerly.

"Yesterday," Stephenson replied dryly.

"Yesterday?" Oliver repeated, baffled.

"Yes, yesterday. Do you think you can make that?"

Oliver shook his head. He had a sinking feeling.

Stephenson spread his hands. "I'm terribly sorry. As I said, only the best candidates make it. You failed, but you got closer than most. You're promising, but not quite enough. There's still some work to be done on your sense of time and your temporal attitudes. Good luck, Mr Wells."

"Thank you, Mr Stephenson."

Oliver left the office and went back home in despair. Damned, he thought. I should have prepared my move better and come earlier. Maybe next time—or should that be the previous time?

The end

J im put down his newspaper as he saw his wife Janet walk past him, on her way to the kitchen. She shot a warm and loving smile at her husband, curled up in his comfy chair, and halted as she noticed he wanted to say something.

"I've been reading a very interesting article here about the future of the sun. It's quite fascinating. Have you read it?"

"No, I haven't, darling. What does the future have in store for the sun then?"

"It says here that the sun will expand until it becomes a gigantic red star, many times its current size. Before it reaches that stage, our planet will warm up dramatically and all life will perish. Ultimately all the inner planets, including the Earth, will be swallowed by the sun."

"Really?"

"Yes, but we're not talking about the near future here. We still have a few million years ahead of us. Even so, I find this notion of the sun destroying everything it is now nurturing thought-provoking. It's a very philosophical idea."

"What do you mean?"

"Well, it means for instance that all our efforts for the preservation of nature, the protection of endangered species, and our ambitions to live in harmony with the ecosystem are doomed. It's all bound to be destroyed anyhow. So why do we bother? Everything we do is pointless. Mankind's days are numbered, whatever we will or won't realize it."

"What do you think we should be doing then?"

"Maybe we shouldn't make such a big fuss about everything. Perhaps we should try to have fun and not worry too much about all that nonsense."

"Well, maybe you're right, Jim," Janet said after a moment's thinking. "In a philosophical sense. We're doomed, so why don't we simply enjoy ourselves and forget all our irrelevant problems? To hell with species facing extinction, with nature, with ecological harmony. Let's do as we please."

"I'm surprised you agree with me, Janet. Usually you don't like that kind of cold scientific reasoning, as you put it."

"That's true, but in this case you had a point, Jim. I have to admit that."

"Well, you should take a look at this article when you find the time. It's well worth reading. Oh, by the way, darling, when will lunch be ready?"

Janet shot him a puzzled glance. "Lunch? Why would I prepare lunch?"

Baffled, Jim stared at his wife, at a loss for words. After a few moments of silence, he managed to say: "You always prepare lunch, darling."

"That was before I learned that we're doomed and that all our efforts are pointless. Maybe I should simply have fun and forget about lunch and all that nonsense."

"Oh, come on, darling. Skipping lunch doesn't seem such a good idea. As a matter of fact I'm a bit hungry already."

"But Jim, try to be reasonable. Mankind will perish, the Earth will be obliterated, and all you're worrying about is missing your lunch? Wouldn't you say your hunger is insignificant in the grand scheme of things?"

Jim simply stared at her, struck dumb. After an uncomfortable silence he managed to say: "You're joking, right?"

Janet didn't react.

"Forget everything I said," Jim continued, his voice edged with stark despair. "Everything."

"You mean the bit about giving up trying to live in harmony with nature? About ecological actions, wildlife preservation, protecting endangered species?"

"Everything, darling, everything. Apart from the bit about lunch."

Janet shook her head. "Men!" she exclaimed. She turned around and went for the kitchen, saying: "Lunch might just be a bit later than usual. Don't worry. It's not the end of the world. At least, not yet. Although it would appear that one day, millions of years from now, the Earth will be—"

"Please don't bring up that subject anymore, darling," Jim said.

"I won't," she said. "Now then, I think I'll prepare lunch."

"Fine," Jim said. "Very fine indeed." The despair had left his voice: hope had been restored. The newspaper was discarded, cast aside on the floor, deemed unworthy of another glance.

Out of sight

It was a typical Saturday afternoon, and as usual George had gone fishing and was enjoying the calm and the opportunity to let his thoughts roam freely rather than the chance to catch a few fish. On this particular day however, the calm was suddenly shattered by a voice seemingly coming from nowhere.

"Good afternoon. Can you hear me?"

George looked around but didn't see anyone. "I can hear you, but I don't see you," he replied. "Where are you?"

"I'm standing right behind you. You can't see me, because I'm involved in an experiment in invisibility. Apparently it's working."

"Really? Well, that sounds interesting. But why did you decide to talk to me? Hearing your voice ruins the effect of your invisibility. Remain silent and you'll be really invisible."

"You have a point there, but at this stage I'm still experimenting. It's good to have some feedback."

"I understand, but we can't discuss your experiment right now. Our talking would scare off the fish."

The invisible man asked a few more questions, but George pretended not to hear him, hoping he would go away. Apparently he wouldn't, and just as the man tried to catch his attention by patting him on the shoulder, George shifted position. The invisible man lost his balance on the slippery grass and plunged headlong into the water. The fish would now definitely look for more tranquil waters. George was furious.

"Help me," the man cried out. Either he couldn't swim, or the cold water made it difficult for him to stay afloat and scramble back onto the river bank.

"I can't see you," George answered truthfully, even if the splashing water indicated unmistakeably where the man was.

"But you can hear me, can't you?" the invisible man shouted desperately.

"You're spoiling the effect again," George replied.

"This is no time for jokes," the man wailed. "I'm drowning."

"All right then," George said. "I'll help you." After all the fish had gone now anyway. Unfortunately he could not see where the man was. There no longer was any movement in the water, the only tell-tale sign of the man's whereabouts.

"Where are you?" George asked. No reply came. Had the man been carried along by the current, or had he succumbed to the low temperature of the water? Or had he followed his advice and decided to remain silent? Being invisible did have its disadvantages.

George sat back down. The calm had returned. Perhaps the fish would return as well. Had all this really happened? He shook his head. What could he do now? Call the police and tell them an invisible man might have drowned here? How were they supposed to find him? He looked around once more and shrugged his shoulders.

He picked up his fishing line again and decided it might be better to forget the whole incident. After all, didn't they say "Out of sight, out of mind"?

Missing

"Mr O'Keefe? Can I have a moment of your time?" Timothy O'Keefe looked through the dirt-streaked window and saw that the man who had knocked at the door was a police officer. This could not be good news. He realized his options were limited, opened the door and said:

"Morning, Officer. Do come in. What can I help you with?"

As the officer stepped inside, Timothy ordered his dog to lie down. "Quiet, Caesar," he said authoritatively. He should try to keep the animal in check.

The officer's eyes scanned his trailer, the dog, his few humble possessions. What was he looking for?

"Can I ask you a few questions?"

"No problem, Officer."

"Didn't you have a visitor here yesterday? A young woman?"

Yes," Timothy said. "A social worker came over to talk about a problem."

"Tell me all about it."

"She told me there had been complaints. Some people here can't accept my way of life. I'm living a simple life here in my trailer, away from the rest of mankind. Caesar here is my only company. I'm a bit of a recluse, you might say. I don't need much, I don't ask anything from anyone, I mind my own business and I accept what nature offers me. It's just that some guys consider part of nature as their property, and when I accept one of nature's gifts, these guys claim that I stole what belongs to them. You might say there was a conflict of interest."

"Yes, Mr O'Keefe, I'm aware of your reputation. Did you and the social worker reach an agreement?"

"That's one way of putting it. The matter has been straightened out. There should be no more problems."

"What happened after your conversation? Did Miss Sanchez say or do anything special before she left?"

Timothy shook his head. Caesar got up and started sniffing at the officer's boots. Timothy licked his lips and said: "All this talking makes me thirsty. Would you like a drink too? I'm afraid water is all I can offer you. And perhaps a little something to eat."

He rummaged in one of his makeshift cupboards, produced two glasses, a jug of water, and a small plate with bits of food. Timothy downed his glass. The officer sipped from his but didn't touch the "appetizers". No doubt he wasn't keen to expose himself to his guest's gastronomic standards—or lack thereof.

"Miss Sanchez is missing since yesterday," the officer finally explained. "We're now talking to everyone she met then, hoping to find some clues. You are one of the last people who saw her. If there's anything you know that might prove helpful, I'd like to hear it. Don't hesitate to get in touch with me if some useful element crops up in your mind later on. We can use every lead."

"I understand," Timothy said. "I'm afraid I can't help you."

"Well, I have to go now. Thanks for your time."

The officer scanned his trailer once more, as if expecting to discover Miss Sanchez's body suddenly, neatly stacked away in one of the cupboards. Then he left and walked back to his car. Timothy threw the rest of the appetizers on the floor, where Caesar quickly gobbled them up.

He downed the officer's glass of water too and shook his head. Weren't the police supposed to find clues and track down missing persons? Apparently they weren't all that good at their job. The officer hadn't even recognized the bits of meat that were all that was left of Miss Sanchez, and he'd had them right in front of him.

Fortunately this time Caesar had behaved himself. That hadn't been the case when that young woman came over here. They had discussed the problem at hand, and then miss Sanchez had made a move Caesar had misinterpreted. The dog, hungry and irritable, had sunk its teeth into her leg before he'd had the time to intervene, and she had screamed. Timothy had made sure the screaming stopped, which might have attracted some undesired attention. And as he and Caesar accepted what nature offered, and nature had been so kind as to offer Miss Sanchez... It had been a while since they had eaten some meat. She made a welcome change from the damned mushrooms and the fruit which he "found" at the market. And it was amazing how much a hungry dog could wolf down. He had tossed the leftovers to the few stray dogs that were always around, and painstakingly removed all telltale traces. Timothy had eaten his share, but hadn't kept too much aside—without a fridge that was rather pointless. Still, the officer had missed out on a rare treat.

He was glad that he hadn't really lied to the officer. He had indeed reached a sort of agreement with the social worker: the matter had been straightened out and there would be no more problems. And there was nothing he could do to help. All his words exactly.

And the officer had no reason to complain. Those guys were tough and hard to stomach. Would he ever realize how lucky he was?

"Murphy's Blues"

The moment Cliff heard the catchy melody he stopped dead in his tracks. He looked around and saw right away where the sound came from. A bit to his right a black woman was sitting in a portico, strumming her guitar and singing the song that had caught his attention. He seemed to be the only one paying attention to her. Most of the shoppers hurrying past hardly noticed the woman's fine performance, and no one even considered giving her some money.

Cliff edged a bit closer to her, trying to understand the lyrics she was singing. With all the background noise of this crowded street lined with shops, bars and restaurants, it was pretty hard to concentrate, but he managed to catch some of the lines. Apparently the song was about a variety of things that could go wrong in a person's life, and that often did go wrong indeed. The words "Murphy's Blues" turned up in every chorus, and Cliff assumed this must be the title of the song.

After some slow and moody picking on the guitar, the song came to an end, and the woman looked up at him. He shot her a warm smile, and on the spur of the moment he groped in his pockets and tossed a few dollar bills into the box at the woman's feet. She thanked him, looked down again and started her next song. Cliff considered moving on, then decided to take an empty seat on the terrace of an Italian bar right across the street. He could use a little rest, and from that vantage point he would still be able to hear the woman sing.

He ordered a cappuccino, and sipped it while listening to the woman's playing and singing. After another bluesy song and an instrumental piece, Cliff was about to get up and leave as he noticed she gave "Murphy's Blues" another go, and he decided to hang on for a few more minutes. When she was halfway through the song some strange things occurred.

A dog crossed the street and slipped between a young woman's legs, making her lose her balance. She fell, dropped her bags and all the goods she had bought spilled onto the street where a car driving past crushed them. A man on a bicycle who had seen the incident failed to notice a group of young girls who had just bought ice cream cones and rode straight into them. They shrieked and managed to get out of the way just in time, but not without losing all their ice cream.

In the meantime a man trying to help the woman who had fallen back to her feet accidentally ripped her blouse apart, leaving her half naked. A guy on the terrace next to Cliff took his video camera to record this string of bizarre accidents, but in his hurry he knocked over his beer, and the liquid spilled onto his girlfriend's lap. As he apologized and started cleaning up the mess, his camera dropped to the ground, and the waiter who just walked past tripped over it, and lost his balance along with his tray of drinks.

Cliff could hardly believe his eyes. How could so many things go wrong in just a few seconds? It was unreal, a scene from a Hollywood movie. He finished his cappuccino and left, glad that nothing had happened to him. He crossed the street and saw the black woman had risen to her feet and was ready to leave too. She shot him a smile and looked him in the eyes, as if she expected him to say something.

"Did you see all that?" Cliff asked.

"Yes, of course," she said. "It was all part of my act, you know. This was 'Murphy's Blues' as it should be performed."

Cliff chuckled. "You did all this? Really? Well, that's some kind of act. At least I'm glad nothing happened to me. Thanks for not including me in your act."

"You have only yourself to thank for that," the woman said, apparently in all seriousness. "You gave me some money. And you were the only one to do so. The universe takes notice of such things, you know."

He stared at her dumbfounded. What was she saying?

"There's no effect without a cause," she explained. "Things happen for a reason. Everything's in perfect balance and there is no coincidence."

He decided to play along with her game. "I thought you just said it was all part of your act? Or maybe the universe is also part of your act?"

She shot him her warmest smile yet and said: "I'm glad you're beginning to see the complete picture. Well, I have to go now. I'll try to find a place to play where more people may be willing to share some of their hard-earned cash. Good-bye, my friend. Take care, and keep in mind what you just learned." The woman turned around and left.

Cliff continued on his way as well. Maybe, he thought, I should make a rule of giving some money to street musicians who are doing a fine job. And simply for that reason. Not so much to avoid Murphy's wrath. After all the woman had been joking. Or so at least he hoped.

Working like a dog

William saw it all happen, right in front of him. He was drinking a beer at one of the many seafront terraces, fully enjoying the relaxed holiday atmosphere, not expecting to see it shattered so brutally.

The seafront was crowded with people, and children were playing and shouting in their shrill voices, and eating ice cream. He counted a fair number of men and women with a dog on a leash, and most of the dogs sported ads on their bodies. Their fur was dyed in the shape of logos and commercial messages, as was so common these days. It was considered easy money, and many people could use that extra income.

From his left, a man approached with a German shepherd, its muscular body adorned with the fluorescent logo of TALK2ME, the hottest telecom operator around. From his right came a middle-aged lady with a small poodle, flaunting a delicate pink ad for BITEWISE, a company offering a hugely successful line of mildly hallucinogenic candy.

Was it the dazzling pink colour that drove the shepherd mad? Had the poodle somehow challenged its defiant counterpart, unlikely as this might seem? Or was it simply a case of "the wrong dog in the wrong place"?

Whatever the reason might be, as soon as the shepherd caught sight of the poodle, it threw itself upon its unsuspecting target as if it wanted to tear the poor creature apart. The poodle proved defenceless against this unleashed monster, and it took the shepherd's owner a while before he could restore the peace. The poodle had only suffered some minor injuries, but little was left of the pink commercial that might have been at the basis of the shepherd's raging fury.

The woman broke into tears, and managed to say in between her sobbing: "Do you realize what your monster has done? It's not just that I'll have to take my little darling to a vet, but how do I explain to BITEWISE that I'll be unable for a while to walk my dog for at least five hours a day in a crowded area with the logo prominently visible? I signed a contract, you know that? I can't fulfil it now, and it's *your* fault. They'll expect me to pay damages, which I can't. Will you make up for that?"

The shepherd's owner replied angrily. "You should have realized this kind of thing can happen and taken out insurance. That's what I did. I'm not taking any chances, even if this cuts into my profits. I'm sorry, lady. I can't help you. I'm not your insurance company."

"How can you be so cruel? Don't you have a heart?"

The man shook his head, and before he resumed his stroll with his shepherd he said: "I have to go now. I can't hang around here for too long. I signed a contract too, you know. I'm supposed to walk back and forth along the seafront for three hours in the morning and three more hours in the afternoon, and I intend to stick to my schedule. I get good money for that. I'm retired and I can use the extra, believe me."

The poor woman was left to her own devices, and tried to comfort her poodle. "I'll have to see a vet as soon as possible," she said. "And then I'll try to have the commercial restored. And on top of that I'll have to pay damages. I'm gonna lose lots of money here. What a horrible day."

The crowd of onlookers dispersed as the woman left the "scene of the crime". A few minutes later everything was back to normal.

William looked up as he saw a young couple approach with a pram. Its sides sported the logos of various baby food and diaper companies. A new outlet for commercials had been discovered. What contract had they signed? How many hours per day were they contractually bound to show off their pram at the seafront or in shopping malls? William hoped that the parents had been wise enough to take an insurance against their children being sick or growing older, as this might lead the advertisers to demand the payment of damages....

A perfect day for a walk

"Would you care for another cup of tea?" Patricia looked her mother in the eyes, frowning with concern, her hands clasped tightly together.

Hovering somewhere between slumber and waking up, the old woman stared back at her, a gaze blank with incomprehension. She remained silent, and merely blinked a few times.

"Would you like another cup of tea?" Patricia tried again.

Now a glimmering of understanding seemed to dawn in the old, greyish-blue eyes.

"Ricia, darling," her mother finally said, her voice a hoarse croaking sound, as if she hadn't used it in years and experienced some difficulties in getting it to work again. "Tea, you said? Oh, I don't know. I suppose I could use some." She struggled into a more upright position, and after a moment's thought she said, "On the other hand, perhaps I'd rather not. Thank you, darling." She turned her head, looked out the window, as if studying what she saw there with deep concentration, and then she added, "I'd rather take a stroll in the garden. It's a perfect day for a walk, darling. Just take a look outside."

Patricia sighed with resignation, and helped her mother out of the comfortable chair she spent most of her days in. "I'll manage nicely on my own," the old woman protested. "I seem to be in good shape today. And I'm sure this little walk will only make me feel better still."

"Be careful," Patricia told her mother as she left the house and shuffled slowly but with unmistakable determination down the garden path. "Take a rest when you feel you're getting tired. And don't stay out too long."

"I'll be all right," her mother assured her. "Don't you worry."

Patricia turned around as she heard her husband enter the room. "Geoff, she's gone out again. I hope everything will work out all right." Geoff came up to her and gently put his arm around her shoulders. "She again said it's a perfect day for a walk in the garden," she added, her voice edged with despair.

Geoff shook his head. "Well, we both know how she is."

"I suppose we'll simply have to wait until she gets back inside. What else can we do?" She leaned on Geoff's strong body, closed her eyes for a few moments. Her mother had become such a burden these last few years. They had considered the possibility of a home for the elderly, but that had proved to be beyond their means, and mother didn't exactly fancy the idea either. ("Nobody will chase me from my own house!") Especially with their son being unemployed and their daughter still going to college, the financial consequences were not to be taken lightly. Still, her mother's deteriorating condition didn't make her and Geoff's life any easier. They could only hope she wouldn't make herself impossible as time went on.

Presently mother came trudging back, beaming with joy. She looked at her daughter and son-in-law, smiled happily, and said, "How absolutely wonderful! I'm enthralled!" She lowered herself into her comfortable chair, leaned back and carefully stretched her legs. "The leaves rustling in the wind," she said dreamily, "the birds chirping, the sunlight finding its way down between the foliage, the sound of children playing and cheering merrily nearby, it all makes for such a *peaceful* neighbourhood. It makes me feel so happy. Why don't both of you go and take a stroll as well? It's a perfect day for a walk, believe me." Her breathing slowed down, a telltale sign that she was about to doze off again.

Patricia locked eyes with Geoff, then cast a glance at the bleak expanse of grey where they had just seen the old woman stumble around. There hadn't been any trees or flowers for over a decade now. Even the grass had withered and made room for dirt and sand and rubble, matching colours with the invariably overcast sky. Every now and then military airplanes flew by overhead, their thundering roar shattering the ghastly quietness and making the houses tremble on their foundations. The effect of widespread pollution, toxic waste dumps, and a few major environmental catastrophes, combined with the civil war and its generous use of defoliants and various chemical and bacteriological weapons had totally escaped her mother.

"Birds," Geoff murmured. "Children playing. Sunlight."

"You know she still lives in the past," Patricia said. "She still sees things as they were in the good old days. That's what keeps her going, what keeps her from going mad."

"I suppose you're right," Geoff said. "And I wonder what will keep *us* from going mad."

Catch a last breath

"If this experiment is successful," Dr Williams explained, "its outcome will revolutionize our notion of time, our grasp of the very nature of the universe and our place in it. We will be writing history. Shall I?"

His assistants merely nodded. Dr Williams hit the "enter" key on his keyboard and sat back.

"There we go," he said. "We should feel the effects of the experiment within moments."

"What exactly do you expect?" his principal assistant asked.

"There's no way to know," Dr Williams patiently replied. "As you know, we are changing the nature of time. We are speeding up time by chopping off a bit of every minute, if you allow me to put it unscientifically. Time is now running in segments that grow increasingly shorter. It will be fascinating to see how we will experience this effect."

They all waited a few moments, but nothing seemed to happen. Dr Williams finally broke the silence by saying:

"The change we introduced in the fabric of time is gaining momentum. Soon we will—"

The assistants shot him a worried look. Why had Dr Williams left his last phrase uncompleted? That was very much unlike him. One of them chose to ask a question.

"Dr Williams, isn't it possible that we fail to experience any effects for the simple reason that we—"

"I think that we are just starting to experience the effect this experiment has on—"

"The segments of time are getting shorter. We'll have to use short—"

"Yes, short sentences. And even then we seem to—"

"Normal communication will soon become—"
"It's not just speaking, even breathing is—"
"We're gasping for air after barely—"
"If this goes on we may well—"
"Is there no way to stop—"
"There's just no time to—"
"We can hardly—"
"Breathing is—"
"Can't we—"
"There's—"
"We—"
"I—"
Silence.

The dark invasion

Timothy rose from his comfy chair and took a good look around his room. To his dismay he noticed it was still remarkably dark. It had been like that for a few days now, and he found this situation quite unsettling.

He shook his head and thought, The darkness is unmistakeably gaining ground in my room.

He considered calling his daughter so she could see the evidence, but decided against it. She didn't like to hear complaints from him. She had told him repeatedly that he should be glad he could live here on the second floor of her house in his old days, rather than pining away in a nursing home. He was no longer able to live on his own, and when his wife had died a couple of years ago, he had been offered this opportunity that he had grabbed with both hands.

So he was grateful to have relatives who took care of him, but they wouldn't put up with all his "silly complaints" about "problems that didn't exist anyway".

So when he had noticed the advance of the darkness in his room, he had chosen not to mention that fact to his daughter. He assumed she might blame it on his failing eyesight or his imagination running wild, and discard this nonsensical idea of his.

And yet he was sure he had stumbled onto something serious and ominous. Ever since he had noticed his room was getting darker, he had kept track of the advance of this phenomenon.

He had tried to fight it by switching on the lights earlier than usual, and by having several lights on rather than just one, even if his daughter frowned upon this "waste" of electricity—there were bills to be paid, and they were big enough as it was.

He went to the bathroom and returned to his chair, but not before checking the situation. Yes, under the bed and in the corners especially the darkness was accumulating, no doubt about that. Were those places bridgeheads of an upcoming invasion that would eliminate all the light? And how could he resist this take-over?

I'll have to think, he said to himself, and sat down again.

He awoke a while later. I must have dozed off, he realized. He cast a glance outside the window and saw that the sky was turning dark. He checked his watch, and shook his head. It's too early for nightfall, he thought. Something's wrong here.

The room too was way too dark for this time of day. I'd better switch on the lights before things turn really bad, he decided. He rose from his chair and flicked the switch. To his horror nothing happened.

He tried the switch again, but in vain.

It's probably just a technical problem, he thought, trying to control the panic welling up inside him. I'll quickly replace that bulb. He always kept a few spare bulbs around, just in case.

A few moments later he tried the switch again, but still to no avail.

I should have known, he realized, that replacing the bulb wouldn't do. There was nothing wrong with that bulb. This is something else entirely. The forces of darkness have launched their final offensive. They're moving in like an unstoppable tide and will take over. Soon light will be a thing of the past.

And there's nothing I can do about it. The darkness will conquer my place and reign unopposed.

He sighed and sank back into his chair, feeling utterly desperate and vanquished. Darkness had won so easily.

❈

"How's your dad?" Ernest asked. "Did he panic?"

"I don't think so," Cindy replied. She had gone up to see how her father had reacted to the power failure, short as it had been. He wasn't getting any younger and often acted strangely when something unexpected happened. She was quite worried by his declining mental condition.

"I don't think he noticed anything," she continued. "I found him asleep in his chair, with all the lights out. He must be dozing off all the time. And he's still wearing his sunglasses. He's had them on for a couple of days now. I have no idea why. As far as I know his eyes aren't all that sensitive to light."

They lapsed into silence, thinking about the issues of advanced age.

Frozen in time

The man next to me at the bar suddenly turned his head towards me and said: "There's something I'd like to tell you. I've recently made an astonishing scientific breakthrough. After years of painstaking research, I finally managed to develop a technique to stop the flow of time. This will be a milestone in the history of science."

"Really?" I replied politely. "I'm impressed. Please show me how you do it."

"No problem." The man seemed to concentrate, stared me in the eyes and simply said: "Look. I froze time."

"So how can this technique be applied, what possibilities does it offer?"

"I froze time," the man repeated. Had he heard my question?

I asked him a few more questions, but each time he simply repeated, "I froze time."

I shrugged, went to the toilet and as I came back I noticed he still hadn't moved an inch. I overheard him saying "I froze time" to the man at his left.

It was very clear to me that the time freezing technique was of limited interest and would not quite prove to be the milestone its inventor had hoped.

The Apocalypse

It had been raining all day, but I had to walk the dog urgently, so I decided to go out for a short stroll anyway. I put on a raincoat, armed myself with an umbrella, and left, ready to brave the torrential downpour. Usually I went for long walks, allowing both my dog and myself some fresh air and a little exercise, but this time I felt a ten minute effort should be enough.

As I passed the small square in front of Saint Christopher's Church, I noticed a man standing there in the pouring rain. He didn't wear a raincoat, nor did he have an umbrella. He just stood there, soaking wet, as if he enjoyed the dreadful weather. I shook my head, wondered what drove this man to do this, and walked on.

Ten minutes later, as I had come full circle and the dog had done what was expected, I thought, *Why not check if the man is still standing there in the rain?* It turned out that he was. As the rain had diminished somewhat in intensity, I decided on the spur of the moment to have a short chat with the man. I just had to know what he was doing there. Of course, he might say it was none of my business. On the other hand, he might appreciate a conversation.

So I walked up to him, and said, as casually as possible: "Good afternoon."

"Good afternoon," he replied. The rain was running down his face in rivulets, and he looked as if he were standing under a shower, his scraggly hair glued to his head, his clothes soaked.

"May I ask what you're doing here in the pouring rain?" I asked. "There's a few pubs in the neighbourhood where you can find shelter. I can tell you how to find them."

"I appreciate your help," the stranger said, "but you needn't worry about me. I will be fine. As a matter of fact, that is exactly why I'm standing here."

"What is that supposed to mean?"

"You may not know this, and most people may not know this, but today is a very special day, and this precise place is a very special place. I'm not standing here by coincidence. I'm standing here because I'm convinced it's the only way to be saved."

"I beg your pardon?"

"Allow me to explain," the man offered, no doubt having seen the expression of bewilderment on my face. "I've had premonitions. I've been given indications. Information has been passed to me, probably coming from God himself. I studied this information, tried to interpret it, cross-checked it with the holy scriptures, and drew the conclusions that seemed inevitable."

"What are you driving at?"

"If my interpretation is correct, only those individuals that happen to be here, at this particular place and at this particular point in time, will be saved, whereas all the others will be struck down. I was called, so I came. I will be spared. I'm sure you understand that, considering the importance of the situation, the rain does not matter."

Right, I thought, we're having a religious nutcase here. Well, that did answer most of the questions. "It strikes me," I remarked, "that you're alone here. Were you the only one who was called? Are you the only one who will be saved?"

"I must admit I don't know," he said. "Maybe I misinterpreted the information I was given. That is a thought that indeed occurred to me. I can only hope that if I'm wrong, the Lord will forgive me."

"And the rest of us will perish?"

The man nodded. "The Apocalypse will spare no one, apart from the chosen ones who have gathered here."

"Unless you misinterpreted?"

The man didn't reply. He closed his eyes for a moment, opened them again and said: "Please, leave me alone now. I wonder indeed why no others have gathered here. But then again, maybe I'm the only one who deserves to be spared. So be it. I'm sorry for the lost souls like you who will pay the highest price for their unwillingness to accept the directives from above. Please, leave me alone now."

I granted him his wish and left, just as the rain began bucketing down again. As I was about to turn a corner, I cast a final glance at him, and prepared to go back home. At that precise moment, I saw how a BMW appeared at the other side of the square, driving at reckless speed. The driver lost control of his vehicle on the wet cobblestones, and the car skidded off the road and onto the square. The man who was still waiting there for his ticket to salvation didn't stand a chance. His body was swept aside; the poor soul must have died on the spot. The car came to a screeching halt against the façade of Saint Christopher's Church.

As I produced my cell phone to call the police, I thought: Well, the victim had received some valuable information after all. Unfortunately, he had misinterpreted it. The Apocalypse would come only for those who were at that particular place at that particular point in time. Everyone else would be spared.

I told the police a serious accident had happened, and a man had sadly lost his life. I decided not to add that the information on the Apocalypse had been poorly formulated and consequently had been misunderstood by the chosen ones.

The garden where time crumbled to dust

"Harry," Vanessa called out, "I think it's still going on," but the wind, feeble as it was, carried away her words to where her husband couldn't possibly hear them. She sighed, and tried to ignore the fatigue her body was suffering from her short walk in the garden. If even this short a walk was already too much for her... Did this mean her condition was getting worse? And could this in its turn mean a change was manifesting itself?

She shook her head, as if trying to shake off the conflicting emotions that disturbed her peace of mind. Anger, hopelessness, uncertainty. And, she'd better admit it, her failure to understand. The strict and total impossibility to know what on earth was happening to them. She just had to talk to Harry about it, regardless of what he was up to at this moment.

Slowly she walked down the gravel path to the patio where Harry was always sitting. No doubt he had dozed off again. His waking moments seemed to be growing ever more scarce. If this went on she would be truly alone soon, accompanied by a perennial sleeper. Unfortunately she knew of no way to stop this process. With unsettling intensity, the realization dawned on her: what did this evolution mean, and what did the very fact that there *was* an evolution mean? It was simply mind-boggling. She just had to talk to Harry about it, right now, even if this meant raising him from his slumber. On the other hand, she had never been so bold as to disturb his sleep in recent times. It seemed so unwise. Who knew what the consequences of such a desperate act might be?

"Harry? Are you awake?" Her voice, already brittle with age, trembled with concern. Maybe she shouldn't wake him. She had only done so a few times, and that was so long ago she couldn't even remember the last instance. It had turned out to spoil his temper, his appetite, his entire day.

To her relief she noticed she had worried in vain: Harry had just risen from his "short afternoon nap" as he preferred to call it in a natural way, and now looked at her with barely-focussed eyes.

"Yes, of course I'm awake," he said, and reached out for his cup of tea beside him on the table. He brought the cup to his lips and took a sip, then gently put the cup back down.

"It's still hot," he said approvingly. "You see? I can't have dozed off for a long time. How else could my tea still be hot?" He looked her triumphantly in the eyes, a faint smile creasing his lips.

"You're obviously right," she said after a moment's hesitation, not without difficulty. Would he never understand? Would he never do so much as notice? Would he never listen to what she had been trying to explain to him on so many occasions? Perhaps it would be wiser to give up altogether, but he took the initiative out of her hands now by saying, "You wanted to tell me something, darling?"

She sighed. "Yes," she said, her voice as steady as she could muster, "there's something I'd like to draw your attention to. I've been keeping an eye on the flowers, Harry, and I've noticed something strange, something unsettling."

Harry closed his eyes, and for a moment she feared he had gone back to sleep. But then she heard him murmur, "Oh no, not again. Do we have to go through all that again?"

"Harry, please. I have this feeling it's of tremendous importance."

"Well, all right then, darling. I'm listening. Please tell me what you have discovered." She could read the expression on his face: weariness, because he was convinced these discussions were leading nowhere, courteous acceptance of her insistence to let him know about her findings, resignation at the inevitability of all this.

"Everything in the garden has stopped growing for a considerable stretch of time by now. The grass, the flowers, the trees. They all stay the way they are. It's as though time has come to a standstill. I had noticed before how it all seemed to be slowing down, but now it appears to have stopped altogether. I don't understand it, Harry."

"But darling, there's no need to worry. How many times do I have to tell you that it's all in your mind? Everything's just fine. It's all perfectly normal. Why don't you take it easy, sit down and have a cup of tea?"

He poured the two cups full of tea, set the pot back down with a deep sigh of satisfaction. He closed his eyes and whispered, "Oh darling, if only you knew how much I cherish these peaceful moments we have here." He didn't reopen his eyes, and after a while his slow and regular breathing told her he had gone back to sleep. Vanessa left her tea untouched, went inside the house, and wandered aimlessly through room after room, all drenched in silence.

The entire house felt cold, as if nobody had lived here for a long time. Yet there were no signs of neglect or poor house-keeping, not even a thin layer of dust covering exposed surfaces. The house was deprived of human warmth simply because it had actually been empty for a long time. There was just the two of them, and Harry had been in his chair on the patio for too long to remember, whereas she had been in the garden, keeping a watchful eye on it, enjoying its atmosphere, and basking in its breathtaking splendour.

Carefully she walked up the flight of stairs leading to the bedroom. She cringed at the slight creaking of the stairs. Even a faint sound like this seemed to shatter the deep silence. The bedroom appeared to be even quieter and more devoid of life than the rest of the house. She felt a mixture of shame and embarrassment for disturbing the serenity as she crossed the room to the window, gently pulled aside the heavy curtains and gazed out at the garden below. Her eyes gradually lost focus and she barely noticed what she was looking at as recollections came flooding back of how it had all evolved this way.

It had been a very slow process—so slow she had not been aware of it at first. It had started when Harry had retired and all of the daily routines and pressures could be discarded. Rising early had no longer been required. Regular hours had become unnecessary. At last they'd had the time and the freedom to sit back and enjoy the days as they came. Slowly they lost contact with the world outside—and to be quite honest, at the time neither of them really cared. Society had been changing so quickly, at a pace they had always found hard to keep up with. The moment it had no longer been necessary to match its pace, they had been all too glad to let the reins slip from their fingers. Soon it had become impossible to catch up with society at large.

As they grew older, the chasm between the two of them and the rest of the world grew wider. It might have been different if they'd had any children. But, sadly enough, that was not the case, and now it was of course too late to rectify that situation. So their lives seemed to slow down. There were ever fewer matters to lend a sense of activity to their days. The housekeeping chores were attended to by a cleaning woman once a week—in recent times she also did all the shopping.

Harry spent more and more time on the patio, reading and drinking tea. As time passed, the quantities of tea increased, and his reading material dwindled away. She had spent more and more of her time in the garden. Time went by—only it passed ever more slowly, until she had discovered it had by now ground to a virtual standstill.

She couldn't remember the last time the cleaning woman had come—although it wasn't apparent from the condition of the house. Harry seemed to be frozen in his favourite time of the day. He took a nap in his chair on the patio, sipping his tea every now and then. Tea-time now stretched into infinity. And in her garden nothing ever grew or changed anymore. Each time she talked to Harry about it he had replied she merely imagined things were wrong. It was all in her mind, he kept saying. He relied on his tea as conclusive evidence, as it didn't cool down, so the eternity she had lived through was in reality obviously but a few moments. It was no use indicating the flaw in his logic. By the time she had explained that the hot tea was part of their surroundings which were now frozen in time, he had usually gone back to sleep. But then she couldn't rule out the possibility that he was right. If, as

107

he claimed, it was all in her mind, then how could she possibly determine the true nature of things?

Of course, there was always the garden. She clearly had not imagined what she had discovered there. But was there a way to convince him of her findings? Was there any undeniable proof for her theory? If only she could bring him to go along with her in the garden, see for himself how...

She shook her head, as if waking up from a maddeningly bizarre daydream. She refocused her eyes, and saw what she had been staring at, however unseeing.

The garden! She had been standing here looking out over it for a number of minutes, and only now she realized perhaps she'd better go down and take a walk in her garden, just to check if everything was all right. Maybe the lawn needed to be mown, some dead leaves had to be removed, the hedge needed cutting or some other task might have to be carried out.

All the recollections swept at once from her mind, she crossed the bedroom, descended the stairs and walked straight into the garden, inhaling the invigorating late afternoon air. At first glance everything appeared to be perfectly normal, but then she noticed with rising concern that there hadn't been the slightest of changes since her previous visit. Flowers that were about to spring into full bloom were still in that state of their metamorphosis. A broken, dying leaf about to drop to the ground was still poised exactly in that position. And these cases weren't exceptional. A closer inspection taught her that this was the general state of affairs. Her garden was no longer subject to change, to the passing of time. This could only mean...

She would have to talk to Harry about this.

The big power failure

"What a beautiful night," Jesse said. "And just look at the stars. Breath-taking."

"You're absolutely right," David agreed. "If only we could stay here forever."

"I don't think we can do that, not at the room rates charged by this hotel," John remarked, and they all burst out in laughter. "Still, this is a wonderful place," John admitted.

Suddenly the lights went out, plunging the poolside bar of the Mandalay Hill Resort Hotel in a semi-darkness broken only by the faint glow of the candle on the table and the stars shining overhead.

"Oh, not another power failure," David moaned.

"Power failures are quite frequent here in Burma, and in other countries in the area. We'll just have to get used to them."

"I know," David said. "It'll only be a few minutes. Let's enjoy the starlit night, now that we can admire it in its full glory."

A minute later the lights came back on, and the men picked up their conversation. Jesse had just started one of his traveller's tall tales as the lights went out again. A sudden gust of wind also extinguished the candle, leaving the stars as their only source of light.

The lights came back on and went out again several times in the next fifteen minutes, and Jesse sighed and said, "This is one of those days, you know. So what do we do?"

"There's little we can do," John said. "We could retire to our rooms, but the power failures will cause us more problems there than here outside. Let's just wait until everything gets back to normal."

"I'd say that's a good idea," David replied.

A few seconds later the stars also winked out, leaving the men in total darkness.

"What the hell is this supposed to mean?" Jesse asked.

"It's probably just clouds that hide the stars," David offered by way of explanation.

"It's a cloudless night," John countered. "The sky is perfectly clear. Anyway, clouds don't come rushing in and cover the whole sky in a split second like this."

"But the stars don't go out like this either," Jesse said. "They're not affected by power failures. Not even in this country."

"So why aren't they shining?"

"I don't know," Jesse said. "Doesn't anyone have a lighter? We could use that candle now."

"I'm afraid we're all non-smokers. We'll just have to wait."

To their relief, the lights came back on a few minutes later and the stars re-appeared in the sky as well.

John looked up and said: "Well, they seem to have sorted out the problem up there."

"Don't be ridiculous," Jesse snarled. "Can anyone offer an explanation for what we witnessed just there?"

No one could, and as he didn't feel like continuing his tall tale, the men sat staring silently in front of them.

Just as Jesse was about to propose retiring to their rooms, the lights went out again, and a few seconds later the stars winked out too.

"Oh no," he said. "It's happening again. What's wrong with the stars? They can't go out like that. This is simply impossible."

"But it just happened, didn't it?"

"Yes, but I'm afraid I can't offer an explanation."

"We're just groping in the dark," John said, chuckling, the only one to appreciate the irony in his choice of words.

"You're all sounding like disembodied spirits, with your voices coming from the total blackness," David remarked, his own voice coming from the blackness as well.

"If this goes on, we'll really end up disembodied," John retorted.

"I really think this is something serious and I'd like to know what's going on," Jesse said.

"Here's my theory," John offered. "This is the Big Power Failure. All we can do is hope He'll get his system back on-line soon."

"You're not funny," Jesse said.

"Let's just wait until everything gets back to normal," David proposed.

They waited, but nothing happened. The darkness was complete. Apparently the system had crashed in a serious way, and the big system up there as well, however illogical that might seem.

I suppose John may have been right, Jesse thought. This is the Big Power Failure. My God, how will this end? So what do we do? Just wait? What else is there for us to do?

So they all waited. And kept waiting.

Incomplete information

"Look!" Frederick Dubarry said, pointing at the scene of devastation below them. "The Golden Gate bridge, gone! The Oakland Bay bridge, swept aside! Fisherman's Wharf, washed away! The Financial District, gone forever!"

"There's just no trace left of San Francisco," Oswald confirmed with a broken voice. "What a disaster!"

"Everyone knew a really big earthquake would hit the city one of these days," Dubarry said. "We just didn't know it would be today. And we all expected to be notified in advance."

"Well, we were," Oswald countered.

"Yes, but everyone thought they would have the time to evacuate. I don't think many people had the chance to get away in time. I was lucky I could catch hold of you. I happened to think of that balloon trip we did last week, remember?"

Oswald nodded.

Frederick Dubarry shook his head. He still couldn't believe it had all happened. The warning that an earthquake was imminent, and that it might be the dreaded Big One. The chaos as people desperately tried to leave the cities on the West Coast, and ended up on clogged roads and in overflowing airport terminals. And his recollection of last week's balloon trip. So he'd called the guy who did the bookings, and arranged for a trip right away.

They had barely lifted off as the quake hit San Francisco, buildings crumbled and fires erupted all over the place. As they were still shocked and awed by the extent of the destruction, a gigantic tidal wave washed away the smouldering ruins and turned the landscape into a raging sea.

"Look, Oswald," Dubarry said. "It wasn't just San Francisco that disappeared under the waves. It must be the whole coastline,

112

maybe even the entire state of California. There's just no land in sight. This is incredible. This must have been the most powerful earthquake in recorded history."

Oswald merely nodded.

"It's the biggest catastrophe that ever hit mankind," Dubarry went on. "I doubt anyone made it alive. The people on the road or waiting at the airport for flights that never took off didn't have a chance. But I survived it, thanks to you. I'll pay you a little extra, on top of what we agreed. You definitely deserve it."

"Thanks," Oswald said flatly.

Dubarry kept staring at the raging waters below them, until he noticed the balloon was losing altitude.

"We seem to be going down," he said, alarmed.

"We can't stay in the air forever," Oswald explained.

"What's that supposed to mean?"

"This is a hot air balloon. Without hot air—" Oswald pointed at the gas cylinders and then at the water below them.

"Hey, wait a minute," Dubarry shouted. "This wasn't part of the deal."

"The deal was to get away as quickly as possible," Oswald said in his defence. "You wanted to be up in the air right away. You said nothing about landing. I'm sorry."

"So I supplied you with incomplete information. Is there nothing we can do then to keep this thing in the air until we're above firm land?" Dubarry yelled furiously.

Oswald pointed at the gas cylinders again. "I'm terribly sorry."

"What will happen when we hit the surface?" Dubarry asked.

"I don't think we'll stand a chance," Oswald answered matter-of-factly.

Frederick Dubarry cast another glance at the raging sea extending as far as the eye could see, and saw that they were about to hit the water.

He turned to Oswald and just before the balloon splashed down he snarled: "Forget about that little extra money I just promised you."

The big apple

The audience was watching with bated breath. They realized it was a privilege to witness the very first experiment with a matter duplicator.

"Nothing can go wrong," Dr René Delvaux, the scientist responsible for the project said. "We've taken all the necessary precautions. The object we chose to duplicate is an inoffensive one. Even if this experiment goes awry, against our expectations and despite our thorough preparation, all danger is excluded."

He walked over to the copying machine, produced an apple from his pocket and gently placed it on the contraption's "pad A". "If all goes well," Delvaux continued, pointing to the still empty "pad B" at his left, "an identical apple will appear over there. Now then, let's proceed."

He hit a few keys on his laptop and peered at "pad B", anxious to see something materialize. To his dismay and everyone's surprise, "pad B" remained empty, but the apple on "pad A" suddenly made a popping sound and grew twice as big.

"I can't believe this," Delvaux said. "Something must have gone wrong. I fail to understand."

The apple made the popping sound again and grew four times as big as its original size.

"Clearly the problem is more serious than I thought," Delvaux said pensively. "This will require major recalibrating."

The apple popped once more and grew so big and heavy it made pad A collapse. The apple, by now of truly gigantic proportions, rolled against the wall with a dull thud, popped and doubled in size again.

"Shouldn't we get out of here before this thing fills the room completely and squeezes us dry against the walls?" someone asked.

"There's no cause for panic," Delvaux said, his voice edged with concern. Understandably the entire audience rose to their feet and stormed out of the room. The last man to leave saw how the apple grew so enormous it made cracks appear in the wall and the ceiling.

"Stop this thing before it wrecks the room," he shouted hysterically.

"Before it makes the entire building collapse," another man added.

"What if this process can't be stopped? Will this thing destroy the whole block? All of New York?"

"The entire country? The planet?" someone asked, chuckling.

"I hope you guys are joking," a woman remarked.

By then we were out on the street and briskly walked away. A heavy rumbling made us turn our heads and we saw the building behind us go down in a fountain of brickwork and dust. Ominously, the gargantuan apple towered above the ruins. Apparently it just kept growing in size exponentially, and we ran as fast we could.

The expanding universe

As Jennifer walked through the room her husband Harold, ensconced in his comfy chair as usual, looked up from his magazine and said: "I'm reading a fascinating article here. Maybe you should take a look at it too."

"Really? What's it about?"

"It's about the expansion of the universe, explained in layman's terms."

"Oh, Harold. I wish you could bring up some more interest for the everyday things of life. Such as the household work. Not to mention our marriage."

"Please, Jennifer, don't start that argument again. I wish you would show some more interest in science and the really important things in life."

"Are you saying that our marriage is of minor importance to you?"

"That's not what I said."

"It would explain why our marriage seems to be heading the wrong way."

"I have no idea what you're driving at, darling."

"It's all in the article you were reading, Harold. Maybe you should reread it more carefully. You'll find the explanation for what's going wrong with us."

Harrold stared at her, struck dumb.

"Jennifer, what are you talking about?"

"Harold, listen to me. What's happening with us proves that expanding universe theory of yours."

Harold kept staring at her and she added: "It explains why we're drifting apart, a process that will only accelerate and lead to its inevitable outcome."

116

She headed for the kitchen, leaving Harold pondering the remarkable symmetry between astrophysics and his marriage.

Beyond the final chapter

Felipe cast furtive glances all around him. There were few people out on the streets, as he had hoped. It was dark, there was a cold wind and rain came pouring down at regular intervals: an ideal day for what he had in mind. The chances of being seen and recognized were slim. He felt confident this would turn out well.

He pulled his hat a bit further down over his eyes, and briskly walked into the arcade. There were a few people there, mostly young men, but they were totally immersed in their video and computer games and did not pay any attention to him. He paused, allowing himself a few moments to adapt to this bizarre environment, all whirling and flickering darkly-coloured lights, nerve-wracking sounds—an artificial universe where chaos and high-tech wizardry were locked into continuous battle, and where humans were but insignificant elements, pitiful blobs of flesh and blood, attached to glimmering hardware, as if desperately trying to coalesce with the metal and plastic, to establish a new kind of symbiosis and renounce their organic heritage.

He forced his legs back into action. The "special" booths were at the back, his friend Jacques had told him. There would be no problems. Nobody asked questions here, as long as you paid good money. At the back there was indeed a man behind a counter. Felipe walked up to him, cleared his throat and said in a muffled voice, "I'd like a 'special'. The 'B' one." As Jacques had said, the man's face showed no emotion. He didn't even look into his eyes.

"That'll be forty-five," a croaking voice said. The guy's lips had hardly moved, as if the words had been recorded and the man had merely pushed the "play" button. Felipe shelled out his money and waited.

"Over there," the man said, pointing at his left. "Just a second. You go in, pick Cubicle Seven, close the door behind you. You'll have five minutes, then you leave through the back door. Make a mess and you pay twenty-five more." Felipe nodded. He wouldn't make a mess; he didn't quite feel like paying seventy. He moved over to where the man had pointed. A few seconds later a door appeared where he would have sworn there had been a computer game. Holographics? Probably. It was perfect for camouflage purposes. He went in, found himself in a dimly lit, narrow corridor. There, Cubicle Seven. He quickly squeezed inside, shut the door behind him and took a seat on the chair, the only piece of furniture in the booth. It was dark and claustro-phobically confining. He stared out in front of him, but as it was still pitch-dark on the other side of the one-way glass, there was only total blackness.

As the light was switched on on the other side, Felipe's pulse rate shifted into higher gear and his hands were suddenly damp. His heart began to throb as if it wanted to leave his thorax. He licked his lips. On the other side of the one-way glass wall (thank God for that!) there was just a desk with a chair. He caught his breath as a man entered the tiny space, clutching a briefcase. He took a seat, opened his briefcase and rummaged in it. Felipe couldn't yet see what was inside the damn thing.

There! Totally flabbergasted, and with hands clamped tightly together and his buttocks at the very edge of his seat so he might drop to the floor any second, he saw how the man took the book (swear to God, a real book, all paper pages with words printed on it, pages flipped over by hand, lines of text scanned by eager eyes, covers gripped with clammy fingers), leaned back, and started to read the damn thing, yes, actually read, and when he had finished a page, a flick of his wrist expertly unveiled another page and he just kept reading. Books. Holy shit, man. Could that really be an actual book? How come it was still around? Everybody knew that the agents from the Ministry of Information were thorough. It was hard to imagine. Could it be then that those rumours were true, about these underground subversive movements, where real books from the old bygone days were secretly guarded and read and circulated? And what could be in those books? What were these people reading, what dazzling ideas went straight into their head? The very idea made him shudder.

Maybe, he thought, it was all a holographic trick—but no, you wouldn't get some state-of-the-art show like that for a measly forty-five. This had to be real. Goddamn fucking real. Felipe swallowed. God, he thought. Jacques was right. This is incredible. Books. There's still some around. Or at least one. But doesn't that mean...

The man at the other side of the glass wall closed his book, put it away in his briefcase and left the tiny room. The light went out. Hey, Felipe thought. That can't have been five minutes! But then of course there was no one he could complain to. Not without admitting what he had done. But at least he had seen a man read a book. He still couldn't believe it. It would take some time to let it all sink in.

He got up from his chair, left the cubicle and hurried back outside, hoping no one would see him on his way back home. He would tell his wife it had been a great VR game. He had a complete story all prepared, had even rehearsed it with Jacques. No one would ever find out he had been to an illegal peep show.

God, he thought as he was back out on the dark street, feeling the rain come down on him. My God, what a night. I'll never forget this.

The escalation

Part one

Miranda picked up her phone, called her best friend Murielle and said: "Do you know what happened to me at lunchtime? I had just finished my lunch and was sipping my coffee when a car crashed into the restaurant's wall. No doubt the driver had been speeding and lost control. All the windows were shattered and lots of brickwork and debris were thrown inside. The accident scared the living daylights out of everyone present. Some people started crying and yelling, assuming it was an explosion or some sort of a terrorist attack. You should have seen the devastation. Tables and chairs were overturned, food and drink were all over the place, and people were in shock. A few children were panicking. One kid in particular was inconsolable because his plastic toy car had been crushed under someone's feet. The wrecked toy was a strange mirror image of the car that had caused all the mayhem. Then there was a man who had dropped a bowl of tomato soup, and the woman who had been on the receiving end looked as if she were covered in blood. Some people thought she was seriously injured and rushed towards her to offer help. Another man who had been close to the wall was completely covered in dust and looked as if he had risen from the dead. I was lucky. All I did was knock over my coffee ending up with some stains on my skirt. When the police arrived it turned out the driver was not injured and had simply walked off. They found him some time later in a bar close by. He told them he didn't remember a thing about what had happened and needed a few stiff drinks to forget the whole incident. I guess he had been drinking, otherwise he would have realized there's no need to forget something you don't remember anyway. I suppose he'll be presented with a nice bill. And I hope my next lunch break will be a bit more traditional. And I'd like to finish my coffee."

Part two

During her coffee break Murielle turned to her colleague Monica and said: "Something strange happened to a friend of mine earlier today. She was having lunch in a restaurant when a car smashed into the wall, and debris and shattered glass were flung in all directions. People panicked, thinking it was a terrorist attack and a bomb had exploded. The devastation was beyond description, tables and chairs were blown away and parts of the wrecked car ended up inside the restaurant. A kid had been trampled underfoot and was crying in pain, and a woman looked as if she was covered in blood, but she was helped immediately. Then there was a guy looking like a corpse, brought back to life. My friend herself just had a ruined skirt, so she can't complain. The police found the culprit later in a bar, downing some drinks as if nothing had happened. I guess they'll make him pay for what he did. Still, this must have been a terrifying experience for all those present there, especially the kids."

Part three

Later that evening Monica was talking on the phone to her friend Melanie while commuting back home.

"Listen, I heard this weird story about something that happened to a friend of a friend. She was having lunch in a restaurant when she heard an explosion. It turned out someone had driven his car straight into the wall, wrecking the whole place and ending up inside. The floor was covered with debris and shattered glass. Everyone was panicking, realizing they were victims of a terrorist attack. Some peopled were covered in blood and required immediate medical care, there was a guy who appeared dead, but fortunately he could be reanimated, and kids were trampled underfoot. It was an absolute nightmare. How can this sort of thing happen here in this country? Where are we still safe? Anyway, my friend's friend survived it all and at least she can still tell her story. I believe they found the guy who was responsible for the attack. He was hiding in a bar in the neighbourhood, and the police managed to arrest him. He'll pay for his crimes. Isn't all this terrible, Melanie? Can't we even go out for lunch in safety anymore?"

Part four

Late in the evening Melanie made a call to her sister Mabel and said: "I heard about a terrible accident that happened today. For some reason it wasn't on the TV news tonight. I don't understand why. Maybe they're trying to cover it up, unless it's a hoax. But I wouldn't be surprised if they were hiding information from us. Anyway, there was a terrorist attack in a restaurant downtown around noon. A guy drove his car straight into the restaurant and ran off just before the vehicle exploded. The damage was considerable and panic broke loose. People were covered in blood, children ended up trampled underfoot, and many suffered mortal injuries. I believe some people didn't make it. The terrorist, who had miraculously escaped, was later arrested by the police, but he refused to yield any information. I wonder why this outrage didn't make the TV news. Maybe they think it might cause a panic? Could that be it? Anyway, I find this absolutely terrifying. I'm not sure if I'll leave the office at noon tomorrow. Maybe it's better to stay safely inside, but then again, who knows where the terrorists will strike next time? We're living in dangerous times, Mabel. How will this end?"

Part five

Just before lunch break, Miranda received a call from her friend Moira, who said: "I'm sorry, Miranda, but I don't think it's a good idea to have lunch together today. I'm terribly sorry for pulling out at such short notice, but the thing is, I'm scared."

"Scared? What for?"

"I was told there was a terrorist attack in a restaurant yesterday. It wasn't on TV or in the papers because they're trying to avoid a panic, at least so I was led to believe."

"Are you serious? What happened?"

"A terrorist drove his car straight into a restaurant, where the vehicle exploded. All hell broke loose, as you can imagine. The place was completely destroyed, people were bleeding to death, and children were trampled underfoot. Medical teams arrived shortly afterwards and did what they could to save lives. It must have been a nightmare come true for all those people. The terrorist apparently managed to escape, miraculously, but the police caught him in a bar. I hope he'll be hanged."

"Are you sure about all this, Moira? I can hardly believe it. And why would they try to cover it all up? They can't do that, can they? Lots of people must have seen or heard what happened."

"I don't know, but I'm too scared to go out for lunch today."

"Well, I understand. We can go some other time."

"Fine."

"You know what's so strange about all this, Moira? Yesterday I was having lunch at a restaurant in the neighbourhood, and there was also an incident with a car. It wasn't serious, though. Just a guy who had been drinking and crashed into the wall. The damage was limited and no one was injured. I got away with a few coffee stains on my skirt. So I shouldn't complain. Who knows what might have happened if I had been in this other place where the terrorist attack occurred? My God! I shouldn't think about that!"

Success/Success

"Dr Stevenson," the nurse said. "I think the patient in room 451 is regaining consciousness."

"Room 451? That must be Mr Fleetwood. I'll be right there."

Dr Stevenson hurried towards his special patient's room. All the EEGs, tests and scans had indicated that the operation had been successful, but it would be interesting to check on Mr Fleetwood himself, thus adding a personal touch that was so important in these matters.

As he entered the room, he thought: Would the patient confirm what the tests had shown? Had the so-called "personality transplant", as the media referred to it, typically and unscientifically, been truly successful? Would the high precision brain surgery he had performed, swapping specific host brain tissue, in a state of deterioration, for pristine donor brain tissue, a medical procedure still in its experimental stages, indeed prove to be the crowning glory of his career?

Let's ask the man, he said. Let's check if the old and impaired "personality" has indeed been replaced by the new "healthy" one, without any interference or disruptions. Let's hear it from nobody but Mr Fleetwood himself.

Mr Fleetwood's eyes were indeed open and he smiled as he saw the doctor. Quivering with excitement and expectancy, Dr Stevenson asked: "Good afternoon, Mr Fleetwood. How are you?"

Mr Fleetwood's smile widened and he answered: "We're fine, doctor. We're getting along nicely. How can we thank you?"

Fatal dimension

The stranger entered the bar, took a seat on the barstool next to me and ordered a beer.

He took a swig from his pint, turned to me and said: "Good evening."

"Good evening," I replied. "How are you?"

"I'm fine," he said. "May I ask you a few questions? I'm curious about this place."

"This bar?"

"No, this world. You see, I'm a traveller through the dimensions. Each world I visit differs from the previous one. In one world Vincent van Gogh was hugely successful during his lifetime; in another John F. Kennedy wasn't murdered; in yet another the Vatican was destroyed by a huge meteor."

"Really?"

"So I'd like to know what makes this one stand out from the others."

"Frankly, I have no idea. I've always lived in this world. I wouldn't know in what way it differs from other dimensions."

"I see your point. Your view is limited. You have no way to compare. But I can. I'm an experienced traveller by now. Let me see a newspaper and I may tell you right away what makes this place different."

He quickly read a paper the bartender gave him and looked up triumphantly. "This is it. There's a reference here to the death of Saddam Hussein. In my home dimension he's still alive and well, and ruling over a vast empire that's still growing bigger. And meaner, because the guy is the worst dictator in recent history. His secret police is eliminating everyone who might be a menace for this tyrant's reign. And believe me, those guys are efficient and they're everywhere."

"What did you say there?" the bartender asked. "The worst dictator in recent history?" He suddenly produced a pistol and shot the traveller. The man dropped to the ground, bleeding from a mortal injury. We all stared at the bartender, shocked by this totally unexpected violence.

"That guy was right," the bartender explained matter-of-factly. "Saddam's secret police forces are efficiently eliminating subversive elements, and they *are* indeed everywhere. And not just in his home dimension. Now, who would like another drink?"

Nature rules

"Really, Uncle Philip, you're looking great. How has it been?" I hadn't seen my Uncle Philip since Aunt Alice had died, half a year ago, as I had been abroad for my company.

"I'm doing okay," he said. "There were some tough moments in the beginning, with the house feeling so empty and cold, but I managed to overcome those problems. Life goes on, you know. You needn't worry about me. I'll be fine on my own here. Would you like some tea or coffee?"

"Tea will be just fine, thank you."

"I'll make some right away. Why don't we go out on the patio? It's such a beautiful day."

"Great idea!"

A few moments later we were both sitting on the patio, sipping our hot tea, talking on a variety of subjects. When our conversation ground to a halt, I rose from my chair to take a look around in the garden, which Aunt Alice had always tended so lovingly and passionately, raising gardening to the level of high art, and ultimately transforming her garden into a many-faceted jewel of flowerbeds, shrubs, and trees. I would never forget all the times that I played there as a child, chasing butterflies, gathering fallen apples in the grass or simply roaming through its multi-coloured splendour and richly-textured fragrance.

As the image of the garden as I recalled it from my younger days dissipated and I grew aware of the garden's current appearance, I put my cup down on the table next to my chair and hesitantly took a few steps forward, astounded and disbelieving. My faint hope that I was staring at a mirage, a hallucination, or an optical illusion proved false.

"Uncle Philip," I stammered. "What on earth has happened to the garden?"

I pointed at the grass that had grown knee-high, and the weeds that had sprung up everywhere, rivalling and often surpassing the grass in height, the vanguard of an unstoppable army of vegetation out to conquer all it found on its path. The colourful flowerbeds, arranged and tended with so much love, had been completely swallowed by this green tide washing over the garden, allowing only the shrubs and trees to break island-like through the surface of waving and rippling stems.

Ivy and other climbing plants had embarked on an offensive from the other side, leaving the trees little hope to escape unscathed. Although their fruit still shone brightly in the late summer sun, it was clear the trees were fighting a losing battle against the deadly invasion coming from two fronts.

The garden had become a miniature jungle, where the strong smothered the weak in a continuous battle for supremacy. I understood right away there would be no more calming walks here, no more harvesting sprees of apples and peaches, no more soothing relaxation on the lush grass under the foliage of a majestic tree.

"Nature must have its way," Uncle Philip finally answered. "Isn't gardening a way of curbing nature's normal processes, an unnatural drive of mankind to impose his own maniacal lust for control and power on Mother Nature? After your aunt passed away, I decided to hand back the reins to good old nature, fully confident in her time-honoured method to run things."

"But, Uncle Philip, the garden is falling prey to chaos!" I protested. "Before you know it it'll be a jungle! The fruit-trees will vanish under the climbing plants, there will be no more flowers, everything that's beautiful and delicate is doomed!"

"That is precisely nature at work, Jonathan. This is exactly what I meant with refraining from the need we feel to control nature, to impose our egotistic views and whimsical ideals. Who are we to decide what should survive or not anyway? And besides, what is truly beautiful? Isn't true beauty to be found in strength, triumphant survival, the ability to cope with and seamlessly integrate into the surrounding world? What you're doing, my dear

Jonathan, is favouring the weak and the unfit. Don't you see the basic error in your thinking?"

"But Uncle Philip," I said in a last-ditch effort to lead him back to reason, "I understand you have neither the time nor the ambition to tend the garden, but why don't you hire a gardener to take care of it? Certainly that would not cost all that much, your problem would be solved... and the garden saved."

"My dear Jonathan, you're missing the point completely. This isn't a question of time or money, but of philosophy."

Our exchange of views dragged on for a while, but as Uncle Philip proved totally deaf to all my arguments and quite adamant about the garden's right to degenerate into a small jungle, I finally chose to switch subjects and steered clear of all topics that might give rise to heated discussion or develop, God forbid, into a quarrel.

Later that evening, after our conversation had meandered between a series of rather inoffensive issues, Uncle Philip prepared a light meal for both of us, and we had quite an enjoyable dinner. Afterwards we retired to the drawing room, and had a little brandy. Uncle Philip started reminiscing about Aunt Alice, the good times they had lived together, the long gone days of me and my brother's childhood, and asked about my career, my plans for the future, how the rest of the family was doing and if I would visit them too.

Suddenly he broke off a question in mid-sentence, put down his glass, and frowned.

"Uncle?" I said. "Are you all right?"

"I'm not feeling too well," he said in a soft voice. "I have this strange sensation here—" His voice trailed off, and he pointed at his chest.

"Don't worry, I'm sure it'll pass," I reassured him. "Just take it easy for a while. Lean back and breathe deeply. Is there anything I can do?"

He shook his head, but after a while he moved his hand feebly, as if this was a titanic effort draining the last remnants of his strength, and said, "It's getting worse, Jonathan. Maybe you should call a doctor. I don't trust this. It might well be serious."

I rose from my chair, trying to remember where the telephone was. What could have caused this? There had been nothing wrong with the food; it had been a very light meal. The drinks, perhaps? But Uncle Philip had only sipped a few times from his brandy. Was he by any chance overreacting to a harmless feeling of indisposition, hoping, even if only on an unconscious level, to raise my concern and compassion? Or—an idea struck me.

"On the other hand, maybe I shouldn't call a doctor," I said, and took my seat again. "Didn't you just say nature must have its way? Wouldn't it clash with your philosophy to send for a doctor and impose our egotistic whims on the forces of nature? Wouldn't it be disrespectful on my part to interfere with some natural process, and go against the grain of your convictions?"

For a moment there was silence. "Good heavens, Jonathan," Uncle Philip finally said with a voice edged with alarm. "You can't be serious. Really, I have this definite feeling that it's getting worse. I feel as if I might faint any minute. Believe me, I think this is serious. Now if you could just—"

"But Uncle Philip," I protested. "You can't possibly expect me to favour the weak and the unfit?"

"My God, Jonathan, what if I die here? Be reasonable, young man!" Uncle Philip really sounded desperate now.

"But Uncle Philip, who am I to decide who should survive or not? Shouldn't I refrain from the need to control nature, and rather let the strong, those who are able to cope with life, triumphantly survive?" I looked at Uncle Philip, noticed that he had grown remarkably pale, and had stark despair written all over his face.

"Jonathan," he said in a barely audible voice, his final plea for help in his dying moment—at least that was how it sounded.

I saw life and colour return to his eyes and features as I rose from my chair, and said: "Never mind all that, Uncle Philip. I'll call a doctor right away." I briskly walked to the corridor where I now remembered the telephone was, but before I left the room I turned around and added: "And shouldn't I perhaps call a gardener as well?"

Travel bug

Dr Mortimer Jacobs had now been gone for half an hour, and we started to have serious doubts about the success of his time travel experiment. Most of us had not shared his optimism about the outcome of his foolhardy attempt to prove his discovery of a working method for time travel.

We were about to discuss how to report his disappearance, as he rematerialized on the small stage he had left with equal suddenness half an hour ago. We were both relieved and surprised as he said: "You've all witnessed a scientific breakthrough of major proportions. Time travel is possible. This discovery of mine will change the world."

As he finished his last sentence, he seemed to shimmer, like a mirage in the desert. We were all worried and even scared, and then Dr Jacobs said: "—all witnessed a scientific breakthrough of major proportions. Time travel is possible. This discovery of mine will change—"

For a moment there was silence. Then Dr Jacobs's senior assistant, Edgar Blake, asked: "Dr Jacobs, are you all right? How do you feel? Aren't you by any chance experiencing side effects of your time travel? Are you suffering from time travel jet lag?"

Dr Jacobs didn't seem to have heard the question. He kept shimmering, like an image on a malfunctioning TV, and he said: "—travel is possible. This discovery of mine will change the world. You've all witnessed a scientific—"

"Dr Jacobs, shouldn't you see a doctor?" Blake sounded quite desperate. The bizarre effect grew worse, and Dr Jacobs kept speaking: "—major proportions. Change the world. You've all witnessed. Travel is—"

We exchanged glances, not knowing what to do.

"—breakthrough. Of mine will change. Time. Breakthrough of major—"

Dr Jacobs now seemed to flicker on and off. It was clear the experiment had gone hideously awry.

"—witnessed. The world. Discovery of mine. A scientific. Time. You've all. Is possible—"

"Isn't there anything we can do?" Blake screamed. Dr Jacobs's final words before his image winked out of existence were: "—time—major—change—"

The last pizza

"I really hate your table manners," I said to the man who was just materializing in the pizzeria and floated straight through my table and even through my four seasons pizza.

"Don't worry," one of the waiters remarked. "These guys are mostly harmless. We've had more of them. They're involved in an experiment in matter transmission and there's the occasional glitch in the system. They shouldn't materialize in here."

The man drifted off to my right and assumed solid shape when his feet were still under my neighbour's table. He was stuck and howled with pain as he tore the table apart.

"Sorry for this mess," the waiter apologized. "We'll take care of this."

"It's all done for the sake of science," my neighbour remarked understandingly.

"It looks more like terrorism to me," I countered. "Just look at all the damage."

The bleeding man was helped and led away by a few waiters, and the wrecked table was replaced. My neighbour shook his head and said: "We're lucky it was only the table that this guy got stuck in. It could have been worse."

A few moments later I saw a foot and a lower leg materialize, protruding from my chest.

"There's a thin line between science and terrorism," I cried out in panic. Those were my last words.

Clean slate

Sammy smiled as he saw a group of tourists appear. They came back from Lake Panddhra, where they undoubtedly had admired the beautiful landscape and the ruins, reflected in the tranquil surface of the water, and would now wait at the bus stop to be picked up.

A few other souvenir vendors were also waiting for a new batch of "customers", as this was an ideal occasion. The tourists would just hang around here until the bus came, and they were an easy prey.

He studied the group of newcomers, picked his target and went straight for him, a fat fortyish man, sweating profusely in his drenched T-shirt.

"Beautiful drawings," he said, holding up his "works of art". "Not expensive at all, a real bargain. Three for five dollars. Please take a look."

The man smiled, and glanced at the drawings. "This is very nice black-and-white work indeed," he said. "Did you make these?"

Sammy nodded. "High quality artwork, wouldn't you say? Very reasonably priced. A perfect souvenir."

The man looked at the drawings, all showing details of the Lake Panddhra landscape he had just visited. He nodded approvingly and said: "Well, all right. Twenty dollars. For the whole set. Is that okay with you?"

Sammy was taken aback. Now this was unusual. Normally people had to be convinced, and then they haggled, and finally bought maybe a few drawings for a couple of dollars at most. No one had ever bought his whole stock, and no one had offered him twenty dollars like that. Was this guy stinking rich or just stupid? But what the hell, this was his chance to earn twenty bucks.

"Fine," Sammy said. "Twenty dollars." He handed over his whole stack of drawings, and got a twenty-dollar bill in return. He thanked the man and walked off. There was nothing more to do for him here, as he had no more merchandise. He'd have to make some more.

Back home he prided himself on another victory on the tourists—and this time a highly profitable one. He tried to imagine his victim's face when he would pick up his set of drawings later today, and discover the ink had faded, leaving him with a stack of blank pages. Blank pages for which he had paid twenty dollars.

It was Sammy's way to get even with the tourists for what they had done to his village and his way of life. They had disrupted everything, so he felt he was entitled to seek revenge. This was his method to take out his frustrations on them that did not affect his souvenir selling business. It was a system that worked perfectly and that he was rightfully proud of.

He still remembered the days when life in the village was simple. It used to be a quiet fishermen's village, where people lived and worked in a traditional way. Now the fishermen earned more money by posing for pictures than for fishing. The local economy had been turned upside down, outsiders had moved in and controlled everything, many people had lost their jobs and now had trouble supporting their families. The good old days were over.

So every small victory like this one made him feel good. He reached inside his pocket, took the twenty-dollar bill and held it up like a trophy.

Hey, what the hell was that? He looked at the banknote, turned it around and around again. He rummaged through his pockets, but there was nothing left, so this scrap of paper had to be the twenty-dollar bill. Only now it was blank. It was just a worthless piece of paper. It had been a forged dollar bill, printed with fading ink. Just like his drawings.

Sammy rolled the paper into a ball and threw it away. Hell! He collapsed onto his bed and shook his fist at the damned tourist.

The guy must have known him and his practice. Maybe a friend or a relative had been here recently and had bought some of these fading drawings, and had told him that story. So he had been waiting for good old Sammy to show up and offer his "art" for sale. And that explained why he hadn't haggled and bought his whole stock for a lot of money. A lot of fake money.

Furious, Sammy realized his game was over. The news had spread. He would have to revise his strategy, come up with something new. He would have to start again with a clean slate.

Yes, he thought, thinking of the blank dollar bill and the drawings that must by now also have started to fade away. A clean slate indeed.

The unspeakable act

It had been another hectic day at the office, and Rick knew very well that his work wasn't over yet. If he went about his business quickly and efficiently, he might still have a chance to go to bed early and get a decent night's sleep. He certainly could use it.

As he got home he tossed his coat onto the couch and kissed his wife on the cheek.

"Good evening," the voice-program of his fully computerized house said. Meanwhile one of its autonomous helping-hand-units was already on its way to pick up his coat and put it in his wardrobe.

"You look tired," Linda said. "Any ideas for dinner?"

"What about Italian? I feel like Italian tonight."

"I'll have the kitchen prepare something."

"Fine. In the meantime I'll get the rest of my work done. I'm supposed to have this special report ready by tomorrow morning."

While Linda gave the kitchen detailed instructions about dinner, Rick read out a stream of random thoughts and ideas about his project to his computer, who would eventually edit all the material and produce an elegant, smoothly readable piece. While talking he glanced at the wide-screen at the far side of the room, where news flashes were being shown in between artsy commercials and music videos.

While preparing his final conclusions, he heard Linda ask the computer if there weren't any messages on their answering machine. The computer lowered the volume of the TV and let the tape roll. There were indeed a few messages, but none of any importance to him. He resumed his work, and when the computer finally had all the data it needed he told it to start editing and writing. He would now have to wait for the first draft to be finished. He would then hand it back with suggestions for a revision until he was completely satisfied with the text. Then he and the computer would discuss layout and assorted matters, and within the hour he should have the galleys of the final draft to correct. By bedtime the computer should be ready to start the printing work while he was sleeping. On awakening tomorrow morning he expected to find the 150 copies ordered of the brochure with his report and all the statistical data pertaining to his special project. Right now he had some time on his hands to relax.

"Dinner will be ready in a few minutes," Linda informed him.

"Fine," he said. "By the way, where's Ian?"

"Haven't seen him in a while. Where's Ian?" she asked in her turn, the question being directed to the computer this time.

"He's in his room," the voice-programme said. "I can put him on the screen for you."

"Please do." The commercials were abruptly replaced by a view from their son's room.

"Rick, I think you'd better come and take a close look," Linda said in an even tone, but he had already noticed what had caught his wife's attention and caused her concern. They stared into each other's eyes for a moment, uncomprehending, unable to say a word. After an uneasy silence, he told her, "We'd better go up and talk to him." She nodded and followed him up the stairs, silently.

⊞

"So what's this supposed to mean, boy?" He looked his son into the eye, demanding a full explanation. Ian cast down his gaze, realizing his parents were none too happy with what they had caught him at.

"A creative project," he mumbled, faintly. "For school."

"I see. And what exactly were you expected to do?"

"We were supposed to make a machine. Something mechanical. Something that..." His voice trailed off. It was clear that he didn't really want to pursue this line of thinking. Rick decided to help him.

"You were asked to come up with a construction of your own, right? You were supposed to use your designing and manufacturing software to create a sort of machine or creative project or however they put it. And, my dear friend, what did you come up with?"

Ian remained silent, numbed with shame and embarrassment.

"In other words," Rick pressed on, "what is this?" He pointed at the bizarre object they had seen their son tinkering with a few minutes ago.

"It's a horse," Ian said.

"A horse," Rick said as calmly as possible. "I see." The so-called horse was made of pieces of wood and sticks which had been stuck together with Scotch tape. He had no idea where the boy had dug up this material. It certainly couldn't have been supplied by the computer system. Could it perhaps be trash the boy had picked up on the street? The very thought made him cringe.

"I didn't feel like using my computer," Ian now said, at last finding the courage to supply a full explanation. "I wanted to use my hands. I felt like making something different and do it with my hands. I wanted to make an animal. It felt like the thing to do. You see, dad, I was getting real tired of—"

"That's enough, Ian. Go to bed now. We'll talk about this tomorrow."

They left the room, and went back down the stairs. Linda had taken the so-called horse along, and looked at it with suspicion, as though it was contaminated.

"We'll have to talk to him," he told Linda as they were at last having dinner. "The boy has a serious problem here. I'm sure it's not yet too late and it can still be dealt with. We should be able to help him get rid of this unhealthy attitude of his. And we better make sure we destroy this horrible thing he's made. Before anyone finds out about it. Suppose the neighbours would see it. An animal, of all things. Just imagine, darling."

Linda winced at the very idea. They ate in silence, preferring to avoid this touchy subject for the rest of the evening.

Cowboys of the rubber plains

"I'd like to have a baby," Miranda said. "A baby?" Mike froze. "Yes." Mike shook his head in disbelief, continued to take off his clothes. "Do you realize what you're saying? Do you know what it takes to have a baby?"

"Yes, I do." Miranda sounded utterly convinced.

Mike was now totally naked and reached for his rubber-suit, folded in its hermetically-sealed shrink-wrap. "Are you aware of the amount of red tape we will have to cut through? And anyway, where did you get the idea? You know very well the dangers involved in having a baby these days. Honestly, I fail to see your point. Now if we can just go ahead?" He ripped open the shrink-wrap and tore it away, then began to unfold the rubber-suit.

"Wait a second," Miranda said. "Don't put it on yet. I want to talk first."

Mike looked at Miranda's inviting contours, dazzling in all their nakedness, and sighed with rising despair. "All right then. I'm listening."

"I really think there's nothing romantic about these rubber-suits. You look horrible wearing one and you feel even worse."

"Oh come on, Miranda." Mike felt anger welling up. "Did you think I'm wearing the damn things just for the hell of it? Haven't you read any newspapers for the last ten years or so? Remember a disease called AIDS, Miranda?"

Miranda simply nodded, eyes downcast.

"Perhaps you also remember that the AIDS virus adapted and evolved into a merciless killer, able to withstand any antibiotic, able to transfer itself to other hosts in a variety of ways, carried by sweat or saliva or any other body fluid you would care to mention? Do you remember how *any* type of skin contact became a mortal risk? People no longer shook hands without gloves. Kissing your children good-bye became a thing of the past. Sex had to be carried out with total body protection. Getting married required endless medical tests. The only way to have babies was by being inseminated under controlled laboratory conditions after a horrifying amount of medical and administrative hassles. You can't have forgotten all of that."

"I haven't," she said, her voice a quiet whisper.

"Fine," Mike said, his anger subsiding. In a sense, she was right of course. The rubber-suits weren't exactly big fun, but at least they guaranteed total safety. They completely enveloped your body, isolated you from the world outside, thus removing all danger of contamination. No body fluid or even breath could pass through. The suits had reservoirs for semen and sweat, and came with air supplies for an hour. Some cheaper types had a ten-minute supply—fine if you were into quickies. You also had your fancy models, shaped and coloured as fashion dictated.

"Mike? There's something..."

"Yes?" She had interrupted his flow of thought. Was she finally ready for what he'd come for?

"I'd still like to have a baby. The old way. Throw the rubber-suit away, Mike. It doesn't really matter anymore." Before he could protest, she held up her hand, and asked, "Haven't you heard the news?"

"No, I was on my way to you. What happened?"

"They seem to have discovered that mutant strains of the virus have infiltrated our food chain. They're also in the water, and apparently some types can travel by air."

"You mean..."

"It means you can now be contaminated by eating or drinking or breathing."

"Oh, I see."

"So either we'll all have to wear a rubber-suit with a lifetime air-supply, or..."

"Or we simply don't bother anymore. Yes, now I see what you mean." After a moment's hesitation Mike dropped the rubber-suit onto the floor and kicked it aside. Miranda was right. It didn't really matter anymore. As he noticed her inviting smile, he eagerly reached out for her.

Back to the present

Dr Thomas Whitford realized that this was a historic moment. He shot a final glance at his assistants in the control room, mounted into the time machine and closed the door. Today he and his team would write history: they would carry out the first-ever scientific experiment in time travel. Unmanned try-outs had failed to yield satisfactory results, and he was proud to be chosen for the first manned expedition.

He took a deep breath and concentrated. Countless times he had gone through the routine in the simulator, but now it was for real. With this state-of-the-art machine he would go back and forth in time. The risk involved was minimal—numerous tests had made that clear. He could hardly wait to begin.

He set the controls for a short trip, five minutes back into the past, as per the instructions. If everything went according to plan, the experiment would not last too long. He would make a number of trips into the past and the future, remaining at all times within the cabin. Monitoring equipment would register everything, but there was a porthole offering him a view. All contact with the control room would be impossible until his return to the present.

A green light told him he had arrived. He looked outside, his heart pounding, but all he could see was a black void. He glanced at the data on his monitor screen, and they confirmed there was nothing out there. This was quite unexpected.

Undeterred, Whitford set the controls for a trip a year into the past. Once again he found there was only a void outside, confirmed by the data from the sensors. It seemed impossible that the machine was malfunctioning. Maybe the explanation was, quite simply, that there was indeed nothing out there, however bizarre that seemed to be.

He decided to continue the experiment. He travelled fifty years into the past, a century, ten centuries, but each time there was just this void. Then he started part two of his planned itinerary: five minutes into the future, then a day, a year, ten years. On the spur of the moment he even went as far as ten thousand years into the future, but the black void persisted.

Whitford slumped down in his seat. These were not the results his team had hoped for, but there was little he could do about that. What might be the explanation for what he had witnessed— or failed to witness? Maybe time only materialized at the very moment it happened, and the present was the only actual manifestation of time. So maybe the past only existed in man's memories, and the future only in his imagination. Thus, logically enough, a void extended both before and after the present. This discovery would shed new light on the nature of time, and might lead to numerous new studies and approaches. So in a sense the experiment had not been in vain.

He was now ready to return and set the controls for the present. While he waited he prepared a little speech for his assistants, even if he hardly had any good news. To his shock and horror, he found that the present was also a black void. This was of course impossible. But wait a minute. Maybe the problem was that his definition of "the present" had been too vague: if the present was indeed, as his findings showed, just a minuscule fraction of time materializing in the space-time continuum, then it wouldn't do to give a date and an hour, even down to a minute. A much more precise definition was called for.

But at what exact time had he left for the non-existent past? And how precise should the definition be? Down to a second? A hundredth of a second? An immeasurable fraction of a second? Maybe his problem was that he was unable to define exactly what "the present" was, so he could not set the controls for this point in time.

He tried to refine the settings, but failed to home in on "the present". That particular moment seemed completely out of reach for him. He kept trying, as there was little else for him to do, but it quickly dawned on him his efforts were doomed.

Panting with frustration and disillusion, he leaned back and stared into the black void. I should never have left the present, he realized. Too bad this knowledge comes a bit late. And I can't say this experiment was futile. After all I discovered the true nature of time. That's quite an achievement for a physicist like me. Unfortunately I won't be able to publish my findings and will be denied any rewards and recognition.

He fidgeted some more with the controls, but then abandoned his frantic adjustments. I'm wasting my time here, he thought, and chuckled at the unintended pun.

If life is sacred...

As Tom returned home from his office, he knew he would have to be very careful. He closed the door behind him, took off his coat and made for the kitchen.

"I'm home," he said to his wife Sylvia, who was reading a magazine on the couch.

"How was your day? Are you tired?"

"It wasn't too bad," he said, "but I'm hungry, so if you'll excuse me—"

"How's your cold?" she asked. It was too late. Her suspicion had been aroused. His strong, clear voice must have given him away. Or perhaps his breathing, which had been pretty laboured until yesterday. He should have known, should have prepared this confrontation more thoroughly.

"I'm feeling much better, really. Now, I'd like to fix myself a quick dinner, so—"

"Tom." He didn't like that special ring to her voice, and sighed as he saw her put aside her magazine, rise to her feet and come towards him.

"Yes?"

"Let me fix you something, Tom."

"I can take care of that myself, honey. This is very kind of you, but really—"

"I find it only normal that a woman should help her sick husband."

"I'm no longer sick, darling." There. He'd said it. I'm a damn fool, he thought. Here I am, taking precautions so my wife doesn't find out I've got rid of this cold and I'm barely through the door and I blow it.

She nodded. "I can see that."

"I think I'm developing a natural immunity against these viruses," he said, in a last-ditch effort to save his hide.

"Oh, Tom, please," she said, "don't be pathetic. I know you've been seeing that dealer again. Tell me, Tom. You've been buying drugs again, haven't you?" She shot him a cold, piercing stare that chilled him to the bone.

He tried to come up with an excuse, an explanation, a story that would get him out of this predicament, but he quickly realized it was no use. She knew. It was too late. "Yes," he admitted. "I'm sorry. It won't happen again."

"That's what you said all the other times. You'll never learn, Tom."

"I'm sorry to hurt your feelings like this, honey."

"You did a lot more than simply hurt my feelings, Tom. I take this as a direct insult. By buying that stuff on the black market you mock me and my work and everything I stand for. And you haven't limited your purchases to drugs, have you?"

"I'm not sure I understand what you're talking about," he said, although he knew all too well what she was referring to. Could it be that she had discovered his bootleg goodies, well-disguised as they were? My God, he thought. This is getting worse every day.

"Let me refresh your memory," she said, her voice cold as ice. He followed her into the kitchen, saw her open the fridge and produce two boxes. "Any idea what this is, Tom?"

His heart sank. It would be no use to feign innocence, but on the other hand...

"On the label it says—" he began, but she interrupted him mercilessly.

"Never mind what it says on the label, Tom. I know how these black market peddlers camouflage their wares. Let me show you what's inside these boxes, Tom."

She dropped them to the ground, crushed them under her heel, and spread their contents all over the kitchen floor.

"See? It's meat, Tom. Dried meat. Cleverly disguised illegal stuff. And you bought it. And you would've eaten it. A quick dinner. Yes, indeed. How can you be so utterly disrespectful of life? Don't you have the faintest glimmer of understanding? Life is sacred, Tom, remember?"

"I know, honey, I know. I just wanted to get rid of this damn cold and I was fed up with this vegetarian food you've been forcing down my throat, and—"

"Tom, please!"

She turned around and strode out of the kitchen, kicking his precious dried meat—bought with hard-earned money—all over the place. It was his own fault, of course. He shouldn't have married a girl who had become a die-hard militant of Sacred Life, a movement lobbying for total respect for all life-forms on earth. As their influence had spread to the highest political echelons, they had managed to outlaw the hunting, raising, and killing of animals for food. More recently they had succeeded in banning the production and use of prescription drugs destined to kill innocent viruses and bacteria. There was still a black market, of course, but people dealing in illegal stuff were having a tough time.

"Tom, I've got good news for you." She was back, waving a newspaper into his face. "There's a piece in here you ought to read. It's about us."

"Oh, really?" This couldn't be good news. He swallowed, closed his eyes for a moment, then said, "Tell me. What's the good news?"

"It looks as if Sacred Life will achieve one more of its goals, Tom. We're heading towards our next success. The battle continues, and we're still gaining ground."

"Fine," he said, not sure if he wanted to know what Sacred Life's latest victory was.

"We're pushing the boundaries of total respect for all life-forms once more," she said triumphantly. "Soon you won't have to eat all this vegetarian food anymore. All plant-life will be protected from man's unrelenting hunger. Crop-raising and harvesting will be notions of the past. Fruit-trees and vegetables will finally be allowed to live their lives untouched by man. We'll do fine with synthetic food. Well, Tom? Don't you think this calls for celebration?"

"Absolutely," he said, numbed with despair. "I'll have a glass of water. Before you people manage to ban consumption of that precious liquid as well."

The deceit of dreams

"Listen to that racket," Gordon said, standing at the window and staring at his neighbour's house. "How can those people stand it?"

"It's music," Samantha replied. "Rock music. Some people happen to like it."

"Well, I'm not one of them," he retorted. "And then there's those kids. They're not exactly quiet either."

"What do you expect from young boys? They're playing and making a little noise. Aren't you exaggerating a bit, Gordon? Take it easy."

"I guess you're right," he admitted, trying to calm down.

"Dinner will be ready in a few minutes. Just relax."

Samantha disappeared into the kitchen and he shifted his eyes again to his neighbour's place. His girlfriend was right. He was overdoing it a bit. It was just that he couldn't stand Mr Carpenter. The man had everything: a decent job, a nice house, a Mercedes parked in front of it, a good-looking wife, two kids...

Everything he didn't have.

Good old Gordon had to make do with a boring desk job, a modest apartment, public transport, and hardly any money left to start a family. It simply wasn't fair. But maybe all that would change now. He would talk it over with Samantha after dinner.

When they had finished their meal they sat down in front of the TV. As Samantha reached for the remote control, he said: "Wait, don't switch it on yet. There's something I'd like to show you."

She shot him a quizzical glance. He held up the booklet he had bought at a bookstore during his lunch break, and handed it to her.

"This may be of help," he said.

She leafed through it and said: "This is a joke, right? *Dreams Come True, or How to Change the World by Dreaming.* What's this supposed to mean, Gordon?"

"It's a manual. This booklet explains how you can actually change things through controlled dreaming. If handled expertly and correctly, dreams may unleash a powerful force most people aren't even aware of. It's all described in detail here. I'll give it a try tonight."

Samantha shook her head. "Oh, Gordon, what a horrible crackpot theory. How can you buy this crap? This is sensationalist nonsense for superstitious fools. Don't tell me you take this seriously?"

"I don't know, Samantha. The bookseller told me this manual had something going for it. And it wasn't all that expensive. Why not give it a try then?"

"So what would you like to change?"

Gordon pointed at the window. "I'd like to stop that noise outside. And put an end to everything else that bothers me about that guy."

"This is ridiculous," she said, got up and left for the kitchen. "Do as you please then, but leave me out of this nonsense. Tomorrow you'll have to agree it was all pretty pointless and a waste of time. Not to mention a waste of money, even if the book didn't cost all that much. You'll see."

He decided to go ahead with the experiment, regardless of Samantha's disapproval. He opened the booklet, studied the step-by-step method carefully and prepared himself to change the world through his dreams. Determined to give it his best shot, he retired to bed. This would be a special night indeed. And tomorrow morning might be even more special.

The next morning he got up and took a shower. Samantha had woken up before him and she was making coffee as he entered the kitchen. When they had finished breakfast Samantha pointed at the booklet he had left on the table.

"Well, did your experiment work? Did your controlled dreaming change anything?"

"I'll check," he said. He quickly walked over to the window and looked out. To his dismay everything appeared to be as it had always been. The house of their neighbour, Mrs Carpenter, was plunged in total silence as usual. When her husband had passed away, years ago, she had decided not to move, even if the place was way too big for a widow without children.

"Nothing's changed," he whispered. "You were right. My effort was futile. I shouldn't have bothered. As a matter of fact, I can't even remember what I wanted to change. This experiment was a complete waste of time and energy. I've been a fool."

"Never mind," Samantha said. "It's not all that important. We've got other things to think about." She patted her swollen belly. In a few more months they would be happy parents.

"Fine," he agreed. "Well, I'm off to work then." He kissed his wife and left. Presently he was driving his Chevy through the dense traffic clogging the streets. His nonsensical experiment was already fading from his mind.

A tale of patricide and impatience

The haggard looking man stormed into the police headquarters and addressed one of the officers on duty:

"I'm turning myself in. I committed the worst crime a man can possibly commit. I don't deserve to be alive any more."

"So what did you do then?"

"I travelled back in time and killed my father before I was born." The man almost broke into tears as recollections of this horrifying act flowed back.

"I don't think it's possible to do what you just said," the officer replied calmly.

"I know what you mean. By killing my father before my birth I gave rise to a time paradox. By all accounts, logically, I should not be around anymore, and yet—"

"That's not what I meant at all. What I wanted to say was, I don't think it's possible to travel in time. There's no such thing as time travel. Now please, I've got work to do."

"You have to believe me," the man said insistently, then suddenly winked out of existence. The officer stared in disbelief at the spot where the man had stood and asked his colleagues: "What the hell was that?"

"Impatience," one of them replied. "It takes a while for these time paradoxes to sort themselves out."

The reminder

Jeffrey sipped his tea, put the cup back down and stared in front of him. He had the feeling something had slipped his mind. What could it have been?

Wait a second, he thought. Hadn't he prepared something for occasions like these? An idea suddenly occurred to him. His pockets! What if he searched his pockets? He started with his trousers, then his shirt and finally his coat. Of course, there it was. A note, with some handwriting scribbled on it. It had to be something important, otherwise he wouldn't have written it down.

Now where were his glasses? He failed to remember where he had put them. He searched his pockets again, but to no avail. The drawers of his desk perhaps? The kitchen table?

It took him a while to locate his glasses (he had left them in the bathroom), and when he was back in his chair again he wondered why he had brought them. He wasn't reading his newspaper, was he? So why would he need his glasses? He put them away, reached for his tea and then saw the note next to his cup.

Could that be it? He got out his glasses again, put them on and read the note.

It was his own handwriting. *Be aware that your memory is not what it used to be,* the text said. *Make notes of important things, and remember where you put them. This will help you organize your days. Always take your pen and your notepad. They will be most useful now that you're alone. Don't let your failing memory get you down.*

He nodded understandingly and put the note back in his pocket. It was true that he was suffering memory problems, and now that he was alone after poor Margaret's passing away, he had better organize his days as best he could. He should try to cope with his failing memory, not succumb to it. Making this note had been an excellent idea.

Now who had suggested that idea again? He thought for a few moments, then finished his tea and leaned back in his chair.

Life wasn't so bad, even if he felt terribly lonely without his wife. They had been married for... how many years? He frowned as he tried to remember when she had passed away. It wasn't all that long ago, was it? He still saw her face before his mind's eye, but couldn't recall her name right now. He shook his head. How could he possibly have forgotten his late wife's name? Obviously his memory was failing him.

Wait a second, he thought. Hadn't he found a way to deal with that problem? An idea suddenly occurred to him. His pockets! What if he searched his pockets? He searched them and came up with a pen and a notepad. Now what purpose might these serve? He wasn't used to writing notes, was he? Anyway, who would he write notes to?

He put the pen and the notepad next to his cup, and tried to concentrate on the problem that bothered him. Now, what was that problem again? I fail to remember, he thought. I suppose my memory isn't what it used to be. Well, he concluded resignedly, there's not much I can do about that, can I...

www.ingramcontent.com/pod-product-compliance
Lightning Source LLC
Chambersburg PA
CBHW030515260626
47157CB00005B/1745